WEST OF BRIAR TOWN

Terry Gomez

Summers at the Oklahoma farm might be changed forever for Billy if the taxes are not paid. Unless an old farmhand, Billy, and Grandma can get the cotton grown and picked before the farm is to go to the highest bidder at auction. The bug brothers to the rescue!

Library of Congress Control Number: 2014914234
ISBN: Hardcover 978-1-4990-5948-9
Softcover 978-1-4990-5949-6
eBook 978-1-4990-5947-2

This book was printed in the United States of America.

Rev. date: 10/15/2014

To order additional copies of this book, contact:
Xlibris LLC
1-888-795-4274
www.Xlibris.com
Orders@Xlibris.com
633842

Contents

For Madelyn Elanore Gomez

Chapter One

Billy Meets Billy Bug

It was the butterscotch of the day, when the sun was slowly going down and the light gave everything a rich yellow glow. Billy had just stepped out onto the porch and took a deep breath of the cool evening country air.

What is that, a creepy crawler? Billy thought when he saw the small bug sneaking out of the shadow of the porch.

Hey, wait a minute, I think he's looking back at me, Billy thought to himself.

Hey, little bug, I'm gonna get a closer look at you!

Billy slowly hunkered over to see the little bug. Then he *jumped* back quickly.

"Geez! Were you trying to fly up my nose?" Billy shouted. He waved his hands through the air wildly, but that crazy bug landed right on his shoulder!

That's okay, thought Billy, *now I can get a better look at him!* He wasn't a very handsome bug.

"I surely hope you don't bite!" said Billy. Just as Billy was about to shoo the bug away, it lit up like a bright-green neon bulb! Billy stood there in amazement with his mouth wide open.

"How can it be?" Billy exclaimed. "I've never seen a bug like this." He thought, *Could there be more like it?*

Billy thought, *He needs to stay with me! I am going to keep him. I'd better get a jar quick! What should I name such a special bug?* "I think I will name him Billy Bug," said Billy happily. "I will set your jar on the table beside my bed where I can keep an eye on you all the time."

Later that evening, Billy hopped in the bed and looked in the jar and said, "Oh, don't look so sad and worried, tomorrow we'll go back outside, just go to sleep for now." Billy then whispered, "Sweet dreams, sleep tight, don't let the bedbugs bite." He giggled as he closed his eyes for the night.

Chapter Two

Let's Go Exploring

The next morning, Billy woke up early. The first thing he saw was Billy Bug looking back at him. "Come on, Billy Bug, let's go outside!" he said, as he wiped his sleepy eyes. Out to the back porch they went. The screen door creaked as it closed behind them. Billy said, "I'll open your jar, and you can stretch your legs if you want to."

Boy! Did he want to! Billy Bug flew out so quickly Billy could barely keep up with him. "Hey! Slow down, Billy Bug, I can't go that fast!" Once Billy finally caught up with him, he told little Billy Bug to ride on his shoulder for a while. "I need to catch my breath." Billy's feet were cold and wet from running through the grass, still wet from the morning dew. Billy and his new pet bug slowly made their way back home. He was so pleased that his little bug wanted to be his friend.

"I'm hungry, how 'bout you?" asked Billy. "Let's go inside, you can meet Grandma, and we can get some breakfast." Grandma's house always smelled like bacon and biscuits in the morning. "Good morning, Grandma," said Billy. "I brought a new friend in for breakfast today."

"So I see, and what a handsome firefly he is!" Billy's grandma said.

"I named him Billy Bug, Billy after me and Bug because he *is* one." Grandma sat Billy's plate in front of him and began cleaning up a little. "One egg over easy [runny] just the way I like it, bacon, and a biscuit with jelly and butter on one half. I use the other half for sopping up my egg," Billy told Billy Bug. "Grandma also gives me coffee, even though I just turned seven. I like it with lots of cream and sugar."

"So, Billy, what do you and your new friend Billy Bug have planned for today?"

"Well, Grandma, we are gonna go out and do some exploring, just as soon as we eat our breakfast." Billy thought to himself, *Hmmm, I wonder what Billy Bug eats for breakfast anyway?*

"That'll be fine, Billy, but be sure and do your chores and make your bed first," Grandma said.

Billy thought to himself, *Oh brother, I've got a bug for a friend and I still have to do chores.* "Okay, Billy Bug, I'll take you out, and you can wait for me on the front porch. You wait right here in your jar, and I'll be back in a flash."

Billy raced back inside, made his bed in record speed, rushed through the rest of his chores, cleaned himself up, and hurried back to the front porch.

"Here I am! See, Billy Bug, that didn't take long. Let's go down the hill and explore." Billy Bug shot off and flew away from Billy just as fast as he could fly. Billy ran to catch up.

Chapter Three

A Tree in the Woods

"Hey, Billy Bug, where are you going? Wait for me!" yelled Billy as Billy Bug was getting further and further away. Billy Bug flew so fast Billy could barely see him. He flew down to the bottom of the hill and then straight into the woods. Billy wasn't scared, though. He had been through the woods lots of times.

Billy Bug finally stopped at a tree that Billy did not remember seeing before. How could that be when he had been in the woods so often?

The tree was big, old, and creepy-looking.

The bottom part of the tree had bare branches hanging down all around it. The branches were so low they even touched the ground. All those creepy branches around the tree made it look like they were hiding a secret place inside, next to the tree trunk. Billy could not wait to go through the branches to investigate. Billy Bug looked at Billy, and Billy could have sworn that bug *winked* at him! Billy was so excited! All of a sudden, Billy Bug lit up as bright as he could, lighting the way through the tree's hanging limbs. "Wow! Thanks, Billy Bug, you surely do come in handy!" Billy followed the small green glow of his friend.

Billy separated some of the old dead branches so he could squeeze his way through. Once inside, he thought, *Wow, what a great secret hiding place.* It didn't seem real. Suddenly everything grew very quiet; the dirt on the ground was as smooth as silk, and the tree trunk looked huge! Billy Bug flew over to the side of the tree. There was a big crack that made an opening in the tree trunk, just big enough for Billy to squeeze through.

Billy heard the wind begin to blow, making the old limbs sway and creak. Just then, he noticed it was suddenly getting darker outside. Billy could smell the sweetness of rain in the air. He thought there must be a storm coming. *Ka-booom* went the thunder! It was so loud Billy was flat on his belly before he knew what had happened. When Billy hit the ground, multicolored dust puffed up all around him. Billy looked up and said, "Come on, Billy Bug, we better get outta here, Grandma is probably worried." It sounded like a good enough reason to get home. Billy was getting scared and nervous. He didn't know why he felt that way, but he did know that he was ready to go!

Chapter Four

Soaked

Billy squeezed back through the old dead branches he had just gone through. The rain began to pour, and the wind blew hard. Billy said, "Come on, Billy Bug, get in my shirt pocket, fast! Let's go!"

The rain and wind made it difficult to run. Streams of water were starting to form and run down the hill like little rivers. As Billy started to run up the hill, his sneakers started squishing and sinking into the mud. He tried to move quickly, but the wind was pushing him back with such force he was not making much progress. One of Billy's shoes was sucked off his foot in the mud. This did not surprise Billy, as he liked to wear his sneakers without any shoelaces; he thought it was easier to take them off and put them on that way. Billy was troubled by having to go back for his shoe. *I am never going to make it up this hill!* he thought. Billy pulled the shoe, already filled with water, out of the mud and did not stop to put it on.

Finally, he made it to the top of the hill. He could see Grandma on the front porch looking for him. She was wringing her hands in her apron because she was so worried.

"Billy!" she said in an excited voice. "I was so worried about you, out in this storm! Look at you! You're soaking wet." Billy looked in his pocket for Billy Bug. Billy Bug smiled up at him. He was soaking wet too. Billy took him out of his pocket and placed him back in the jar he had left on the porch. Billy Bug shook all over, spraying little drops of water on the sides of the jar.

Grandma said, "Come on, Billy, we'd better get you dried off before you catch pneumonia. Leave your shoes on the porch. Why in the world do you only have one shoe on anyway?"

Billy thought to himself, *I suppose that's what I get for taking my shoelaces out.*

Billy went to his room and put the jar with Billy Bug inside on the table. He put all his wet clothes in a pile on the floor, got a towel, and dried himself off. He got out some dry shorts and a T-shirt out of the old chest of drawers Billy's Grandpa had made; it sure felt good to get out of those wet clothes. "Well, now what, Billy Bug? It looks like we are going to be stuck inside for the rest of the day," Billy said to his little friend. "I want to go back to that tree with a flashlight! Come on, let's go sit on the front porch, and I will let you out for a while." Billy went to the porch and opened Billy Bug's jar. He began to fly around in circles and landed on the porch step beside Billy. Just then, another lightning bug flew over and landed right next to Billy Bug. Billy thought, *Oh my gosh, now there are two of them!* He was so happy to have another bug friend. "Well, what can I call you?" said Billy to his new friend.

"You must be Billy Bug's brother. I think I'll call you Buzz."

Chapter Five

Jake

Jake was an all-around handyman on the farm. He had worked for and helped Grandma for as long as Billy could remember. He was a tall, lanky man who always wore overalls, even to church on Sunday. Only on Sunday he would wear his good "Sunday go to meeting" overalls. Jake had big hands and didn't say much, but he always gave Billy a quarter for candy on sale day every Wednesday. Jake would reach down deep into his front overall pocket and pull out a change holder. It was a small plastic oval-shaped container that had a slit in the middle that would open when he squeezed it to get coins out.

Grandma came out on the porch and said, "Well, Billy, it looks like it's gonna clear up soon. That surely was a heavy rain shower. It should help the cotton. We sure need to get it picked so we can take it to the mill."

When Grandma saw Billy's new friend, she said, "Oh, Billy, now you have two!"

"Yep, I named him Buzz," said Billy.

"So what are you going to do with those bugs?" asked Grandma.

"Whatever they want, I suppose. I was wondering, when the rain stops, would it be OK for Billy Bug, Buzz, and me to have a picnic? We have some more exploring to do."

Grandma said, "Billy, I think that is a fine idea. Let's go ahead and get you packed up. When Jake comes in from the barn for lunch, I'll let him know that you won't be joining us."

Billy said to the bugs, "You guys wait out here, and I'll be right back." They packed a sandwich and a piece of cake, and then filled a thermos with Kool-Aid. Billy went outside and found Buzz and Billy Bug rear-to-rear, having a contest to see who could make the brightest light. Billy grabbed a flashlight and the paper sack with the picnic packed in it. He put on a pair of dry sneakers and said, "Come on, you guys, let's go have a picnic."

Chapter Six

Swimming in Kool-Aid

Billy headed down the hill as Billy Bug and Buzz flew alongside. They stopped at the old tractor at the bottom of the hill. Billy often had his picnics here and would sit on the old tractor parts. He wiped off the rainwater and spread out the feast. He gave Billy Bug and Buzz a cake crumb and began to eat his sandwich. Billy couldn't get his mind off what might be inside the old tree.

Maybe there will be a treasure chest left by pirates hundreds of years ago. I hope there aren't any wild animals or big hairy spiders, he thought to himself.

He took a swig of Kool-Aid from his thermos bottle. The cake was chocolate, with a big, thick layer of chocolate icing. Billy ate it in two big bites. His mouth was stuffed so full he could barely chew. His cheeks were pooching out like balloons. He looked down and noticed Billy Bug and Buzz had done the same thing with their cake crumb!

Billy took another swig of the Kool-Aid from the thermos and poured a little into the lid for Billy Bug and Buzz. They both instantly jumped in and went for a swim. "Hey, you two knuckleheads, that's for drinkin'!" shouted Billy as he giggled at his friends.

I wish I could swim in Kool-Aid! Billy thought. *What a life!*

Billy Bug and Buzz climbed up on the rim of the lid and shook all over to dry themselves. Billy packed everything back into the paper bag and set it on the tractor seat. *We can leave this stuff here and get it on our way back home,* he thought. Billy Bug led the way back to the tree; Buzz rode on Billy's shoulder. Billy squeezed through the dead branches. All Billy could see of Billy Bug and Buzz were small green lights as they flew around under the canopy of the tree's old dead branches. Billy walked over to the side of the tree where the opening in the trunk was and turned on the flashlight.

Billy Bug and Buzz flew in. Billy took a deep breath, stuck the flashlight in, and squeezed his way inside the old tree. He was amazed as it seemed he was looking into another world. It was a huge space, and the inside walls of the tree were covered with something that looked like glistening multicolored sand. The sand glittered and sparkled in the prettiest colors Billy had ever seen: blue, green, yellow, and purple.

Then something *really* amazing happened. Billy Bug flew up to Billy and said, "Well, what do you think?"

Billy looked at Billy Bug in shock, not believing what he had just heard. "That can't be, bugs can't talk," he said out loud. His mind was racing with what to do next. Should he run back to Grandma's house as fast as he could? Pass out? Lie down and kick his feet straight up in the air and die? How could this be?

Billy Bug said, "It's fairy dust."

Buzz said, "Yeah, it's fairy dust." Buzz had a funny, squeaky, high-pitched voice.

Billy Bug said, "You know . . . what fairies use for magic. This is where fairy dust comes from. Come on and I'll show you a fairy."

Chapter Seven

Do You Have Any Secrets?

Billy Bug flew deeper into the opening of the old tree. Billy followed with Buzz riding on his shoulder. Buzz said, "Yeah, come on and we'll show you a fairy." Billy Bug turned a corner, and Billy could hear the trickling of running water. As Billy turned the corner, suddenly the tree was full of light. Billy could see everything. There was a huge waterfall flowing into a beautiful crystal-blue lake. There were green grass, ferns, and flowers that Billy had never seen before. There were butterflies, grasshoppers, toads, lizards, and dragonflies. It was beautiful!

Billy Bug flew over to a toadstool and said, "Come on, come on." Billy bent down and saw a tiny little fairy sitting on the toadstool. She was the most beautiful thing he had ever seen.

She said, "Hello, Billy, my name is Awryn. Welcome to my home. Do you live nearby?"

Billy answered, "Um, yes. I'm staying at my grandma's house for the summer. She lives up the hill."

Awryn asked, "What's it like past the trees' branches? I'm not allowed to go any farther than the top branches."

"It's great, I guess, but nothing like in here," answered Billy.

"Someday, I would like to visit and see for myself," Awryn said. "I see you've met my friends."

"Yeah, I call them Billy Bug and Buzz," said Billy.

Awryn laughed and laughed. "I think I'll call you guys that too!" she said to the lightning bugs. Billy Bug and Buzz looked at each other; Buzz rolled his eyes.

"So, Billy, tell me about you. Do you have any good secrets?" asked Awryn.

"Aw, I don't know. Not much to tell really. I just turned seven, and I am staying with my grandma for the summer in the house at the top of the hill. There's a farmhand named Jake that does all the farming and fixin' for Grandma," Billy replied. "Jake plants cotton and keeps a pretty good-sized garden. He picks the vegetables, and we take the extra stuff to the sale in town on Wednesdays. I get penny candy and root beer in a big mug for a nickel at the drug store. Do you like candy?"

Awryn said, "Well, I really have never had any. Fairies don't eat much. That's why we are so small. So what about those secrets, do you have any?" she asked.

"Well, yeah, but you know how secrets are. You're not supposed to tell anyone," replied Billy.

"Oh, Billy, you can tell me. Silly, you can tell fairies anything."

"Well, I am not sure, but I think Grandma might lose the farm. I know ever since Grandpa died, things have been hard for Grandma, even though Jake tries to help out. She has never talked about any of it with me. But one day when Grandma was gathering the eggs, I heard her talking to Jake. She told him that Bart from the bank said if she did not pay her bank loan by the end of next month, they would take the farm and auction off anything worth selling," Billy explained.

Awryn looked at him and frowned. "Our worlds are very different. I really cannot understand how any of that could happen, but maybe I can help. Why don't you guys come back tomorrow, and it will give me some time to think about it, and maybe I will be able to come up with a plan," she said.

Billy Bug and Buzz flew over to Billy. Billy Bug said, "Yeah, Billy, let's come back tomorrow."

Buzz said, “Yeah, tomorrow.”

Billy said, “Okay, I’ll come back tomorrow if you’re sure it’s okay.”

Billy Bug said, “Come on, Billy, do you remember the way back home?”

Billy looked around and said, “Yeah, I think so, but I’ll follow you. Come on, Buzz, I’ll give you a ride.”

Buzz said, “Yeah, a ride.”

Billy Bug turned the corner and was out of sight. Billy hurried to keep up. He thought about what a strange day it had been and wondered if all this could really be happening.

Chapter Eight

Out of My Gourd

As they were walking back up the hill, they stopped at the old tractor to get the paper sack from lunch. Billy took a big swig from the thermos bottle and poured some in the lid for Billy Bug and Buzz. They both sat on the rim of the lid and had a big drink. Billy said, "Well, now what are we going to do?"

Billy Bug said, "We've got to help your grandma save the farm from that rotten Bart the Banker."

Buzz said, "Yeah, save the farm."

"Awryn will think of something," Billy Bug added.

Billy said, "Maybe I should talk to Jake and see if he has any ideas about how to save the farm. He probably won't even talk to me about it. I sure can't tell him about you guys and Awryn. He would think I am out of my gourd."

I wonder if I am? thought Billy. "Oh, come on, you guys, let's get back to the house."

Grandma met them at the door. "Billy," she said, "we are going to have company tomorrow. Your cousins will be here to stay for a few days."

Oh nuts, Billy thought. *How am I going to see Awryn? What about Billy Bug and Buzz?* Billy's cousins were all older than him, but not by much. Billy always thought his cousin Jessie was a little off in the head. He said bad words, wandered off, and it seemed like he was always in some kind of trouble.

Billy took Billy Bug and Buzz to the side of the house and sat on the cellar door. "Okay, you guys, when my cousins get here, you're going to have to steer clear of them. They will smash you just to *smash* a bug," Billy said.

Billy Bug and Buzz looked at each other and bugged their eyes out. Billy Bug stuck his chest out, stood on his back legs, and flexed his arm muscles and said, "I'm not afraid of any cousins."

Buzz said, "Yeah, I'm not afraid of any cousins. We're not, right?"

Billy warned them again, "Just remember, steer clear of them. I'll try and sneak away from them sometime, and we can go see Awryn."

Chapter Nine

Jessie, Jerry, and Larry

In the early afternoon the next day, a beat-up old pickup truck pulled off the dirt road onto the side of the yard. As the dust settled, Jerry and Larry, the twins, jumped out of the back. Jessie was up front with Uncle Luke. As he was getting out of the truck, he saw Billy coming out of the house to meet them and blustered, "Well, if it's not Silly Billy. What you been doin'?" The twins didn't even say hello as they followed Uncle Luke into the house.

Grandma had caught a couple of chickens for supper the day before. This was always a sight to see. She would run around the yard until she caught one, take it to the old wood block, and then she chopped its head off! Next, she let it go, and the body would run around the yard. Billy hated to see them run all over the yard, back and forth, bleeding everywhere. He was always afraid one would run right into him. He had been staying on the farm every summer for as far back as he could remember, and he never got used to how Grandma could just go out and get a chicken for supper like that. He would always think, "I'm not going to eat any of that chicken!" but he always did, and it was always the best chicken he had ever tasted.

Billy decided to go into the house to see what everyone was doing. Grandma was busy cooking the chicken, some in her electric frying pan and the rest in a big cast-iron skillet on the stove. Uncle Luke hugged her and asked where Jake was.

"Oh, he's down by the river mending the fence, he'll be up for supper shortly, I suppose."

Luke was lazy as all get out. He said, "I think I will go sit out on the porch and wait for him. Let me know when supper's ready." Billy went with the cousins to unpack their clothes and put them away. Jerry and Larry would sleep with him, and Jessie would stay in the guest room.

"When you boys get through, I want you to go down to the basement and get me two jars of green beans and a jar of beets," Grandma said.

They quickly stowed the clothes and went down to the basement. The stairs to the basement were just off to the side of the kitchen. There was a freezer down there, potatoes spread out on the floor, and a whole bunch of old stuff that Billy couldn't exactly identify. There was another room off to the side of the main part of the basement. The room's walls were lined with mason jars of vegetables and fruit and who knew what else that Grandma had canned. There was also a bed in the middle of the room.

The basement smelled like dirt and always seemed cool. Sometimes Billy and the cousins would sleep down there, but Billy could never stay down there all night. He would always get scared and go back up to his room. The basement was okay to sleep in, but it gave him the creeps if all the lights down there were turned off because it was so dark.

He let the cousins go down the stairs first. That way they would have to find the light cord in the middle of the main room and pull it to get the light to come on.

Jessie said, "Hey! Let's sleep down here tonight."

The twins said, "Yeah, we can make up scary stories."

Great, thought Billy. "Come on, you guys, let's get back upstairs and see how much longer till supper's ready." When they got back upstairs, they gave Grandma the jars and asked when supper would be ready.

"Oh, in about twenty or thirty minutes, I suppose," Grandma replied.

Jessie said, "Let's go outside and play in the road."

Chapter Ten

The Race Is On

The road in front of Grandma's house hardly ever had any cars or trucks go down it. The county road grader had been down the road that morning, so the dirt was soft and moist. Jerry and Larry dragged their heels across the road to make a starting line. Jessie said, "Okay, you guys, line up and we'll see who's the fastest. I'll say go." Billy, Jerry, and Larry all kicked their shoes off and lined their toes up on the starting line. Jessie said, "Okay now, wait a minute. I'm gonna mark the finish line." Jessie walked about fifty yards and dragged his heel across the road. Jessie said, "Ready, set, go!" The race was on.

The race was on.

Billy quickly jumped out to an early lead. Jerry and Larry were side by side. Jerry leaned forward and grabbed Billy's shirt to slow him down, and Larry took the lead. Jerry pulled Billy behind him and let go and then tried to catch up with Larry. Larry crossed the finish line first, and then Jerry; Billy finished last. Jessie said, "Billy, you're slow as molasses."

Billy said, "Your brothers are cheaters, everybody knows I'm the fastest runner in the county!"

The fight was on. Jessie lunged at Billy, and Jerry and Larry piled on. Billy was strong for his size and hard to keep a hold on. He struggled and got loose from the three of them.

"I'm not of afraid of any of you," Billy said, breathing hard with his fists in the air. Soon Billy had caught his breath enough to ask, "How would you like a tour of Fist City? Then I got a one-way ticket to Hurtsville for all of you."

They heard Jake yell, "Hey, you boys, stop that fightin' or you're all gonna get a good whoopin'! Come on and wash your hands, it's suppertime."

They all dusted themselves off and headed to the house. The boys crowded around the sink in the bathroom next to Billy's room to wash up. It was the only bathroom in the house. There was still an old outhouse just off the back porch behind the house. There was usually a spiderweb or a wasp flying around in there, and a Sears catalog for looking and wiping. The outhouse rarely got any use, unless you were outside and it was handier.

Everyone gathered around the table for supper. Grandma had already set the table and brought in the chicken, gravy, green beans, beets, mashed potatoes, and biscuits. Grandma's chicken was always crispy and great-tasting. Everyone always filled their plates and ate until they were so full they couldn't take another bite. Jessie always ate his chicken till the bone was clean.

Billy said, "Ew, Jessie, you are not going eat all those veins and yucky stuff, are you?" This only encouraged Jessie, as he made a show out of sucking all the gross stuff off the bone. *He's so gross,* thought Billy.

Whenever there was company at Grandma's house, all the kids did the dishes. The boys split up—one to wash, one to rinse, and the other two had to dry and put the dishes away. Once they finished up with the dishes, they were all ready to get back outside.

Chapter Eleven

Looking for Information and Finding Trouble

Billy Bug and Buzz had an idea of their own. They were going to try to get some information from the grown-ups on what it would take to save the farm. Billy Bug said, "Buzz, let's get into the house and see if we can hear what they are saying."

Buzz said, "Yeah, let's get into the house and see if we can hear what they are saying. Hey, how are we going to get in?"

"Easy, we can squeeze through the crack in the cellar door, go through the basement, and fly up the stairs to the kitchen," Billy Bug answered.

Billy Bug was already trying to squeeze through the cellar door.

Buzz said, "Hey! Wait for me!" And they were on their way.

Billy Bug and Buzz made it to the kitchen, and they could hear Jake, Grandma, and Uncle Luke talking.

Luke said, "Well, you know, it might not be a bad idea for you to move into town."

Grandma looked at Jake and said, "No, Luke, I've discussed it with Jake, and we're planning on staying until they drag us out of here. This farm has been in my family since the Land Run, and I don't intend to just give up and walk away from it now."

Luke said, "Well, then would you mind telling me how you plan on coming up with the five thousand dollars that is due to the bank next month?"

Grandma said, "We have the cotton in the field. If it would just produce, and if we can somehow get it picked in time, we would have the money to pay."

Jake said, "We are trying to do all we can, Luke. I don't see how it can be done either. Even if the crop does come in, we don't have any money to pay anybody to come and help us pick it."

Luke said, "Have it your way. Stay until they drag you outta here. I'll tell you what, though, there is no way that's not gonna happen."

Grandma said, "That's enough, Luke. I don't want to discuss it with you any further. You've never offered to help out around here."

Luke said, "You know I have a bad back. I'm going to go lie down for a while, and then I'm driving back to town before it gets dark."

Luke headed for the kitchen to get one more piece of pie before he took his nap. Billy Bug and Buzz could hear him coming. They got so excited they both turned to take cover and smacked right into each other! Billy Bug said, "Get out of the way!"

Buzz said, "Yeah, get out of the way." They collected themselves and snuck around the back of the counter on their tiptoes until they made it back to the basement door.

Chapter Twelve

Serious Business

Billy and the cousins had decided to go for a walk down the dirt road to the Pettigos farm. It was just a little ways down the road just past the first bend in the road. On the way, they passed a big ravine next to the road where the dirt had washed away and made a big ditch about thirty feet deep and at least sixty feet wide. Billy had named this particular ravine the Valley of Death due to its dangerous appearance. The ravine had an area in the middle where there was a small patch of ground that was still as high as the road. You could walk out to the high patch on a small sliver of land about a foot wide, with a drop off on either side. Walking across was always scary. Billy always thought one of them would surely be killed from falling off. Either that or bitten by a deadly poisonous snake. Neither of which ever happened.

The last time the cousins had come for a visit, Jessie slid down one side of the embankment, and a big pile of dirt came down with him, making a nice soft spot to land. This made for big fun. Now they could all slide down and have a soft landing spot. Billy was afraid at first, but he finally got his nerve up and slid down. They all slid until they got tired of climbing back up the steep side of the ravine.

When they got to the Pettigos, they were met at the door by Minnie. Minnie always chewed Doublemint gum. Billy had always admired the way she could chew and pop her gum at the same time. Billy tried but never could get his gum to pop. Minnie offered them all a stick of gum. She was cooking chicken and dumplings.

They did not stay long. Their mission was accomplished as soon as they got the gum. Minnie must have known all along what their visits were all about, but she always seemed happy to see them. By this time, it was starting to get dark. Uncle Luke had already headed back to town. When the boys got back, they began catching toads and putting them in a bucket. They were using the flashlight Grandma always let Billy take when he went out in the dark. They would shine it up and down the road, looking for toads. The toads would always pee as soon as they were picked up. The boys had to pick them up by their midsections, hold them out, and then drop them into the bucket.

There was never any reason for catching toads other than for something to do. Sometimes they would try and race the toads, but they usually just hopped the wrong way. The toads would be left in the bucket overnight. The bucket was always empty when they got up in the morning. Billy always wondered if they hopped out or if Jake let them go when they went to bed.

After getting ready for bed, Billy asked Grandma if they could have a midnight snack. He always called it a midnight snack even though they went to bed shortly after dark. Grandma would always say "OK," and they would have a glass of milk, cookies, or carrots with water to drink, or something like that. One time Grandma even made them corn on the cob!

The boys headed downstairs to the basement. Billy said, "I'll be right back," grabbed the flashlight, and headed outside. He hurried over to the side of the house by the cellar door. He couldn't find Billy Bug or Buzz, and then he saw a light-green glow out by the chicken pen. Billy ran over and followed the glow to the back of the pen.

Billy Bug said, "Hey Billy, over here!"

Billy said, "Oh, am I glad to see you! I've been stuck with the cousins all day. I can't get away from them for a second, and tomorrow is sale day."

Billy Bug said, "Buzz and I have been busy too. We snuck into the house and heard Grandma and Jake talking to Luke about the farm. Billy, your Grandma needs five thousand dollars in a month, and it does not sound like her chances are too good to come up with that much money in just a month. The crop is in the field, but it has to grow and produce a bunch of cotton, and she has no money to pay someone to help get it picked!"

Billy said, "Thanks, Billy Bug, at least now we know what has to be done. We've just gotta figure out how to help her do it."

"Hey, where is Buzz anyway?" asked Billy.

"Oh, he just went down to the bottom of the hill. There is a dragonfly down there named Sarge that he likes to play army with."

Billy asked, "Do you think you could find him and go and tell Awryn why I couldn't come back to see her today?"

"Sure, Billy, Buzz and I can tell her what is going on, and maybe she will have an idea of how to get a big crop of cotton picked for your grandma," Billy Bug replied.

"Oh, Billy Bug, I'm worried. I don't see how we can help, but we've just got to make everything okay for Grandma," Billy sighed.

Jessie hollered out the front door, "Billy! Are you in the outhouse again? I swear you must have the runs or something."

Billy said, "I've got to go, Billy Bug, I'll try and meet you tomorrow after we get back from the sale."

"OK, Billy, I'm going to get Buzz and talk with Awryn, I'll be looking for you tomorrow," said Billy Bug.

Billy Bug raced down the hill to find Buzz. Buzz was on his belly squirming around like an army man. Sarge was standing on a small mound of dirt. "Buzz," Billy said, "we've got to go find Awryn and talk to her for Billy."

Sarge said, "Would you *be quiet*! You are going to blow our cover. Can't you see we are in the middle of a secret mission?"

Billy Bug said, "How ya doin', Sarge?" Sarge was a big dragonfly, the oldest one anybody around here had ever seen or heard of. His wings were multicolored, and he was always in a bad mood.

Sarge said, "Well now, isn't that fine and dandy? Are we going to have a nicety-nice chitchat here in the middle of a war zone?"

Billy Bug said, "Come on, Sarge, Buzz and I have serious business to take care of here."

Buzz said, "Yeah, serious business."

Billy Bug said, "We may need some help, Sarge."

Now Sarge was very interested. He said, "What kind of serious business could you two have?"

Billy Bug answered, "Can't talk now. We've got to see Awryn lickety-split. We'll tell you more later."

Buzz said, "Yeah, lickety-split, see you later."

Billy Bug and Buzz raced to the old tree and flew through the old dead branches to the side of the tree with the opening. Billy Bug said, "OK, Buzz, now let me do all the talking."

Buzz said, "Hey, how come you always get to do all the talking?"

Billy Bug said, "Now listen, Buzz, this is serious business. I'll tell you what—if I leave out any important stuff, you can tell Awryn yourself."

Buzz said, "Yeah, OK, leave out some important stuff, and then I'll tell Awryn."

Billy Bug rolled his eyes at Buzz and said, "Come on, follow me."

Chapter Thirteen

Cotton Seeds

Billy Bug and Buzz entered the tree through the hidden opening. They flew around the first corner and saw Awryn sitting beside the lake talking to a butterfly. The butterfly's name was Millie. She had huge wings that were white, purple, and blue, and big brown eyes with dark eyelashes and two long antennas. She was so beautiful.

Awryn saw Billy Bug and Buzz and said, "Hey, you guys, it's about time you got here. I was just telling Millie about Billy. Where is he anyway?"

Billy Bug said, "Billy couldn't come today. His cousins have come for a visit."

Awryn said, "Why didn't they all come?"

Billy Bug said, "Oh no, Awryn, we wouldn't want that. The less people that know about this place, the better off we'll all be."

Awryn said, "Why is that, Billy Bug?"

"Oh, Awryn, that is just the way it is. Sometimes people are mean and ornery, and they do things that can hurt bugs, butterflies, and even fairies! That's why you're not supposed to ever fly out past the canopy of the tree's dead old branches. You're always safe as long as you don't go any further."

Millie said, "I'll swear, Awryn, sometimes I don't know about you! Don't you know how dangerous people can be?"

Awryn said, "The only person I ever met was Billy, and he seems nice enough."

Millie said, "Well, a lot of them are not nice at all. Do you know what they do to bugs? They kill them, or even worse, they torture them and then kill them!"

"Oh Millie, stop!" Awryn said. "I can't believe that."

"Well, you better believe it, girlfriend. They even have nets made just to catch butterflies."

Billy Bug said, "All right, all right, Millie, I think we get the picture."

Awryn said, "It's OK, Millie, really. I know Billy would never do anything to harm any of us."

Millie said, "I'm not so sure."

"Millie, you know, we may be able to use your help," said Billy Bug. "Let Buzz and me talk to Awryn and we'll let you know."

"Oh whatever, Billy Bug. What kind of name is that anyway? I'll be in the field. You know where to find me." With that, Millie stood up at the water's edge. She spread her beautiful wings and flew out over the lake and toward the opening in the old tree.

Billy Bug said, "Awryn, Billy has big problems. Buzz and I overheard Billy's grandma talking to Jake and his Uncle Luke. She's gonna lose the farm if she doesn't come up with a bunch of money to pay Bart the Banker next month. Jake has cotton planted in the fields, but it has to produce. I'm tellin' ya, it has to produce a lot, Awryn. Plus she needs help to pick it, get it to the sale, and get the money to the bank on time."

Buzz said, "Yeah, and Billy's Uncle Luke is a no-good, lazy scoundrel that won't be any help."

Awryn said, "You know, I've never seen a cotton field before. I'm not sure what kind of a plan I can come up with that would help. Hmmm, unless . . . maybe if I could go to the field, I bet I could come up with an idea to save the farm!"

Billy Bug said, "*What?* Awryn, you gotta be crazy! You know you can't fly past the dead old branches of the tree."

"What! You gotta be crazy!" chimed Buzz.

Awryn said, "Now wait a minute, guys, I'm not a baby anymore. I'm sure I can go outside of the trees' canopy and get back safe and sound and nobody would even miss me."

Billy Bug said, "No, Awryn, it is out of the question. Anything could happen to you out there."

"Look, are you gonna show me where that cotton field is, or shall I find it myself? You know it would be a lot safer and faster for me to go and get back if you two would just show me the way," Awryn said as she tapped her toe on the petal of a rose.

Billy Bug looked at Buzz and said, "Well, what do you think?"

Buzz said, "Well . . . what do you think?"

Billy Bug said, "All right, Awryn, but we better get going. It will be getting light outside soon."

Awryn was delighted! She said, "Great! Let's get going!" She had never felt such a sense of freedom and adventure before.

Billy Bug and Buzz led the way to the cotton field. Awryn was amazed with the world outside of the old tree. There was so much to see. The sky was dark and yet full of bright twinkling stars. The night air was clean, and she breathed big gulps of it. There was dew on the grass, and the moonlight made it glisten. They flew across the meadow to the cotton field.

Awryn said, "So this is what a cotton field looks like." She was not too impressed. All she saw was a big flat stretch of dirt with long rows plowed into the earth.

Billy Bug said, "Yeah, this is it. It doesn't look like much, but each of those rows is full of cotton seeds."

Buzz said, "Yeah . . . full of cotton seeds."

Billy Bug explained, "As soon as the seeds grow and make cotton, it will need to be picked and sold. If there is a good crop, Billy's grandma and Jake can take it to the mill and sell it. The trouble is they need the money for the farm sooner than the cotton will be ready. Grandma will need a lot of people to come and help pick it too. She doesn't have any money for that either."

Awryn said, "I see. You know, guys, I think I have a plan. But for now I'd better get back to the tree."

They all turned to take one last look at the cotton field to size up the work that needed to be done.

Chapter Fourteen

A Case of the Runs

The first rays of the morning sun were starting to appear on the horizon. They all flew back to the tree as fast as they could go. When they arrived, Awryn said, "See, here we are. Back safe and sound. You guys go and find Billy. Tell him I need to see him soon. I think I can help."

Billy Bug and Buzz flew back to the house. When they got to the old farmhouse, they could smell bacon cooking. Billy's grandma must already be up. They wondered where Billy was. They heard the back screen door swing shut, so they flew around back to see who was going out. They breathed a sigh of relief when they saw Billy heading towards the outhouse. He had decided to go to the outhouse because the cousins were in the bathroom inside taking their sweet time doing who knows what.

Billy Bug and Buzz flew to Billy and rested on his shoulder. Billy said, "Hey, you guys, it sure is good to see you."

Billy Bug said, "Yeah, it is good to see you too."

Buzz said, "Yeah, it's good to see you too."

Billy Bug said, "We have got to talk to you. We have news!"

Billy said, "Come on, let's get in the outhouse before someone sees you guys."

Billy Bug said, "We have a lot to get caught up on. You won't believe what happened last night. Awryn left the tree for the first time ever and flew to the cotton field with us!"

Buzz said, "Yeah! Awryn left the tree for the first time ever!"

Billy Bug said, "You know, Buzz, I am about sick and tired of you repeating everything I say."

Buzz said, "Well, Mister High and Mighty, I am only trying to help you make your point, you dimwit."

Billy Bug said, "OK, Buzz, that does it. Now we're gonna see who is the dimwit around here, and it sure isn't gonna be me!"

Buzz said, "Well, Mister Uppity Up, let's just see who the dimwit is around here."

Billy said, "Would you two knock it off? We only have a few minutes before one of those cousins comes looking for me. What in the world was Awryn thinking about to leave the tree? Just think of everything that could have happened to her. What *did* happen? Why did the three of you decide to go to the cotton field?"

All of a sudden, the outhouse started to rock!

"What is going on?" Billy said. Billy Bug and Buzz hovered in midair in front of Billy's face. Then they heard them. Laughing and laughing and laughing. The cousins had found Billy! Billy didn't know what to do. He couldn't let them find Billy Bug and Buzz. Billy yelled to the cousins, "You creeps get out of here and mind your own business, I got the runs!"

Jessie laughed and said, "You could have used those yesterday when you lost the race to Jerry and Larry!" All the cousins thought that was a good one and laughed even more.

Jessie said, "Come on, Billy, Grandma and Jake want to hurry up and have breakfast this morning so we can get to town. It *is* Wednesday, you know."

"I'll be along as quick as I can," Billy said. He waited until he thought they had gone, and then he looked out a knot hole in the side of the building to be sure. Billy turned and looked at Billy Bug and Buzz and whispered, "OK, you guys, the coast is clear. You gotta get out of here."

Billy Bug said, "Wait a minute, Billy! Awryn said to tell you she wants to see you. She thinks she has a plan to help your grandma!"

Billy said, "She thinks she has a plan! What kind of a plan?"

Billy Bug said, "We don't know yet, she just sent us to get you."

Billy said, "Oh, guys, what am I gonna do? I can't ever get away and be on my own while the cousins are here. Unless . . . I know! You guys tell Awryn Uncle Luke will be here to pick the cousins up tomorrow. Then things will be back to normal. As soon as they pull out of here, I'll be on my way to the tree."

Buzz said, "Yeah, Billy Bug, you tell Awryn Billy will be there to see her as soon as those cousins of his pull out of here tomorrow."

Billy Bug said, "I swear, Buzz, have you ever had an original thought in your life?"

Billy said, "You guys! Don't start it. Remember, you've gotta get out of here without the cousins seeing you."

Billy Bug and Buzz flew out of the knot hole. Billy headed back to the house.

Grandma said, "There you are, Billy. I was getting worried about you. Jessie said you're not feelin' good this morning?"

Billy said, "Aw, Grandma, I'm OK, it's just that those cousins really bug me sometimes."

"Now, Billy," Grandma said, "It is good for you to get to know them and spend time with them. Every summer you're out here with just Jake and me you must get lonely for people closer to your own age."

Billy said, "I sure don't get lonely for *them,* Grandma. A little time with those three goes a long way."

She said, "Now hurry up and eat your breakfast. Everyone else has already finished. I'm going to pack some sandwiches to take to the sale. We'll have a picnic lunch."

Billy poured the cream in his coffee and added two heaping spoons full of sugar and wondered what in the world kind of a plan Awryn could have.

The cousins were outside helping Jake load a five-gallon water jug into the back of the truck. Billy finished his breakfast, and he and Grandma went out to help finish loading the truck.

Jake said, "Finally! What was taking you so long? Are y'all about ready to go?"

"As soon as I get our lunch situated," said Grandma.

Billy climbed into the back of the truck with Larry and Jerry; Jessie rode up front with Grandma and Jake. Jake started the truck and pulled out of the yard, and they headed into town. It was only about a ten-mile drive, but it always seemed to take forever to Billy.

Larry and Jerry played rock, paper, scissors while Billy played possum. He figured if he pretended to be asleep, they would not bother him. Unfortunately, he was wrong.

Larry said, "Hey, Billy, come on and get up. We know you're not sleepin'."

Billy said, "Well, I would be if you would be quiet!"

Jerry said, "How come ya want to sleep anyway? We just got up."

Billy said, "You know I get carsick. I figure if I could sleep all the way into town I wouldn't feel sick."

Larry said, "Billy, you are such a pansy. Why can't you be tough like us?"

Billy said, "Yeah, you two are a couple of tough guys all right."

Jake slowed the truck way down; there was a cow that had gotten out and was standing on the side of the road. As they drove slowly past, Billy looked it right in the eye and said "Mooooah." The cow's eyes got wide, and Billy could see the white that rimmed them. The cow's nostrils flared, then it lunged at the truck. Billy smashed his way through Larry and Jerry to get to the other side of the truck.

"Did you see that?" Billy laughed. "That cow almost hit the truck. I didn't think it would act like that just because I mooed!"

Larry said, "What did you expect, you dumbard?"

Billy said, "Oh man, I am about sick of you two."

Jake pulled into town and stopped at the gas station on the corner. All three of the boys hopped out of the back of the truck. Jesse said, "Let me out, Grandma, I'm going inside too."

Jake reached into his pocket, pulled out his change purse, and squeezed it open. He gave the boys each a quarter. The boys went inside to get some penny candy. Billy always liked to get jawbreakers, the *hot* ones, banana taffy, and bubble gum. He got two handfuls, all he could carry, and placed it on the counter and had the lady put it all in a small brown paper bag. The other boys did the same, and they all loaded back up in the truck.

Chapter Fifteen

A One-Dollar Bill

Jake had finished gassing up the truck and headed to the sale. The sale was in a large, open grassy area with tables set up. Some people sold things out of their pickups. The boys liked to walk around and look at everybody's stuff they had brought to town to sell. Grandma liked to stop and visit with all the ladies, and Jake always headed over to the livestock barn to see the livestock to be auctioned.

The livestock barn was on the north end of the sale grounds. It was a two-story building, and it had a corral. It was painted dark red, and the second floor was much narrower than the first. The entire second floor was surrounded in windows.

Every sale day, there would be a raffle. Billy, Jessie, Larry, and Jerry all went over to watch the drawing. There was a man standing on a platform speaking to the crowd. He looked into the crowd and said, "Hey there, young man, would you come up and draw the winning ticket?"

Billy thought, "Is he talking to me? I can't believe it!" Jessie pushed Billy forward and said, "Get on up there, Billy." Billy stepped onto the platform, and the man said, "OK, son, just stick your hand into the hopper and pull out a ticket." Billy did just that and handed the man the slip of paper. The man called out a name, and there was a hoop and a holler in the crowd, and then the entire crowd started clapping.

A tall, skinny farmer stepped out of the crowd. Billy had never seen him before, but the farmer was smiling ear-to-ear. Billy moved toward the edge of the platform to step down. The farmer said, "Wait a minute, young man. Thanks for drawing my name," and he handed Billy a one-dollar bill!

Billy could not believe it. He looked up at the farmer and said, "Thanks a lot, mister!" Billy's mind was racing; how could he be so lucky? What could he spend all that money on? Maybe he should save it. Maybe he should hurry on over to town and spend it. The cousins circled Billy in the crowd and said, "What did he give you, Billy?" Billy took the folded dollar bill out of his pocket and showed it to them. Their eyes got big, and Jessie said, "What are you gonna do with it?"

Billy said, "I don't know, I haven't made up my mind. Let's go into town."

Jessie said, "Well, let's go!"

Chapter Sixteen

A Nickel Root Beer

After they were done looking around at the sale, they all walked into town, just a couple of blocks from the sale grounds. They went to their usual first stop, the drug store. The drug store had a heavy wood-framed door with glass from top to bottom. It squeaked as Jessie opened it, and they all filed in. The wood floors creaked when you walked on them. To the right was a long soda-fountain counter with round stools. The boys always headed straight for one of the booths that lined the wall at the end of the counter. Each of the boys ordered a root beer. The root beer at Huff's Drugstore cost a nickel and was served in tall frosted mugs.

Larry and Jerry were roughhousing in the booth; Jessie was laughing at them. Billy figured they were going to get into trouble. He knew they would. They always did.

They all finished their root beer, left the drug store, and walked up and down both sides of the sidewalk on Main Street and headed back towards the sale grounds. The noon whistle blew. It was a loud, long whistle that blew every day at straight-up 12:00 noon. It was their signal to meet Grandma and Jake back at the truck for lunch.

When they got back to the truck, Grandma had a blanket spread out and said, "You boys come on over here and get a sandwich before the ants do."

The boys all sat down on the blanket except for Jake. He sat on the tail gate of the truck while Grandma used one of the lawn chairs.

Billy said, "Grandma, guess what? I got to draw the winning ticket at the raffle today, and the man who won gave me a dollar bill!"

Grandma said, "My goodness, Billy, that's a lot of money. I hope you didn't forget to thank him. He surely didn't have to do that."

Billy said, "Sure I did, Grandma. I still can't believe he gave it to me."

Jessie said, "You should have seen Billy when the guy called him up on the stage to draw the ticket! He was scared to death."

Billy said, "I was not, I wanted to do it!"

Larry said, "Yeah right, Jessie had to push him onto the stage!"

Billy said, "I just didn't know he was talking to me when he said to come on up there."

Chapter Seventeen

Cool Wet Sand

After lunch, the boys packed up everything and put it in the bed of the truck and headed over to the grocery store. The small grocery store was on the corner of Main Street. Grandma always did her grocery shopping every Wednesday after the sale. The store was small, and the aisles were narrow. It was difficult to maneuver the cart and for all the kids to stay out of the way. The boys usually got bored with the grocery buying pretty quickly. The store was so small, and Grandma went every week so she usually did not need all that much. She checked out at the register, and all the groceries were packed in boxes. Each boy carried a box back to the truck, and then they were on their way back to the farm.

It was such a hot summer day when they got back the boys decided to go swimming in the river. They all rushed down the hill and headed toward the cool water. They all soon remembered there was no need to hurry; it was always a long, hot walk to the river. Grandma was going to drive the truck down and meet them after she put the groceries away. Jake helped carry the boxes in, and then he went to his toolshed, where he spent most of his time fixing things that needed fixing when he was not working around the farm.

The shed was a long building made out of wood, and it had a tin roof and a dirt floor. There were long tables lining the walls and a few scattered around. All the tables were cluttered with tools, and the shed always smelled just like you would expect a toolshed to smell. It was a mixture of wood, metal, and oil.

The boys were almost to the barbed-wire fence that separated the farm from the river when they heard Grandma coming in the truck. They were hot and sweaty from the long walk. Jessie put his foot on the bottom strand of the barbed wire fence and held up the one above it so they could all squeeze through.

The river was wide, but it was mostly just sandbars this time of year. The water was barely knee-deep in most places except for the swimming hole. Billy went down to the edge of the river to the cool wet sand. If you stood in the same place and moved your feet up and down, the sand would get mushy with water and you would start to sink like quicksand. No one actually ever sunk that Billy knew of.

Grandma had brought the minnow seine and bucket. They could seine on their way back from the swimming hole and hopefully get some minnows to use for fish bait. She left the minnow seine bucket on the riverbank, and they all waded through the river to the swimming hole.

Larry and Jerry ran ahead. Billy took his time. He loved to be in the river, especially on a day like today, when it was so hot outside. When they finally made it to the swimming hole, they all jumped into the deeper water. The swimming hole was not that big and did not allow for a lot of room for anyone. At least they could get their whole body wet at one time. To them it was the greatest. Grandma sat in the shallow part of the river and watched the boys and refereed as needed.

Chapter Eighteen

Catfishing

Jessie decided it would be a good idea to feel around on the bottom for any underwater crevices to find catfish. Billy said, "I hope you catch one because I'm sure not gonna feel around down there. What if there is a big snake?"

Jessie said, "Billy, why are you so afraid of everything?"

Billy said, "I'm not afraid, I just don't want to grab hold of a deadly poisonous snake and get bitten."

Jessie said, "There aren't any snakes in here, you goofball."

Billy said, "Yeah right, like you would know."

Jessie dived under the water to feel around. Billy, Larry, and Jerry waited for him to come back up. Jessie's head popped up, and he said, "I don't feel nothing down there." He continued his bobbing up and down, to no avail.

They were all getting bored with the swimming hole; there was only so much you could do within such a small area. Grandma asked, "Are you boys ready to go and seine for minnows?"

Jessie said, "Yeah, let's go. Maybe we'll catch a big fish in the seine."

They all waded back through the shallow river to the bank where Grandma had left the minnow bucket. The boys unrolled the seine, which had two sticks on each end with a long narrow net attached to the sticks. Billy took one end and Jessie took the other.

They carefully dragged the seine through the water and swung one end around to the bank.

They all lifted the net out of the water just a few minnows and a small perch. They tried again; this time there was a small catfish and a few more minnows. They turned the little catfish loose and kept all the minnows in the minnow bucket.

Grandma said, "That's enough minnows for today, boys. Let's get them home and see if Jake wants to drive over to the pond and go fishing."

They all piled into the back of the truck, and Grandma drove back through the fields toward the house. The road was only two ruts made by the truck. About halfway back to the house, the boys had decided to walk the rest of the way. Jessie was sitting on the edge of the truck bed and leaned around to the cab of the truck to tell Grandma they would walk the rest of the way back. The boys jumped off the slow moving truck one by one and watched it pull away.

Chapter Nineteen

Horseflies Big Enough to Ride

The boys were still wet from the river, so it didn't seem as hot as it did on the way down. They were all walking along the ruts in the road when Larry started swatting at a fly, a horsefly to be exact. Billy's only guess as to why they were called horseflies was because they seemed big enough to ride! Before they knew it, there were horseflies swarming all around them and biting their wet legs and arms. "Y'ouch!" Jerry cried out. All the boys started to run with their arms swinging all around, trying to keep the flies off them. The only good thing about horseflies is that you could usually outrun them. The boys ran until they were tired and slowed down to a walk again. Fortunately the horseflies were no longer in hot pursuit.

There was an apple tree and blackberry vines on the edge of one of the fields along the road. They all decided to walk over and see what was ready to pick. Billy climbed up into the apple tree and picked a few of the apples and threw them down to Larry and Jerry. Jessie could reach up and pick his own. They wiped them off on their wet shirts and gobbled them up. They were tart and made their mouths pucker up; other than that they were good. You always had to be on the lookout for wormholes though. Billy decided he was going to go check out the blackberries. He was almost there when he stepped in the sticker patch. He stood there trying to balance and pick stickers without having to put his foot down and get more. He was stuck in the patch. Jessie came over and held out his arm for Billy to hold on to for balance while Billy tried to pick three more stickers off. At last he was sticker-free and was ready to try and take another step without stepping on more. After a few more steps and a few more stickers, he was finally free of the sticker patch.

Billy said, "Thanks, Jessie." Jessie had come to Billy's aid but not without picking up a few of the stickers of his own.

Jessie said, "Billy, why don't you watch where you are going?"

Billy said, "I *was* watching, it all happened so fast! Before I knew it, I was in the middle of it." Larry and Jerry had carefully tiptoed over. They finally made it to the blackberries. They picked the ripe ones and popped them in their mouths. The berries were sweet and tasted great. They picked all they could eat without getting into the thorns on the vines, and then they headed back over to the road. When they finally made it back to the house, Grandma said, "What took you boys so long?"

Billy said, "We stopped and ate some apples and berries."

Grandma said, "Jake is ready to go fishing, he's going to drive us over to Brown's pond."

They all loaded back up into the truck. After the short drive, Jake pulled off to the side of the dirt road, and they got the poles and minnows out and squeezed through yet another barbed-wire fence. The grass in the field they had to cross to get to the pond was high and golden from the summer heat. Jake had also dug some worms to take along for bait. The boys grabbed their cane poles and headed over to a tree limb that hung out over the pond and started to fish for perch. They never kept the perch to eat; they just liked catching them. The perch were plentiful, and the action was nonstop. Jake and Grandma preferred to fish for catfish, which was a much slower pace. They just dropped their lines in the water and waited. Billy soon became bored with the fishing and decided to go exploring.

Chapter Twenty

Shep as a Pillow

Billy loved to walk along the trail that ringed the pond. The trail had been beaten down to form a rut by the occasional visitor to the pond. Shep, Grandma's old collie dog followed along with him. Billy had always thought Shep was the best and the smartest dog in the world because he knew how to shake. All you had to do was put your hand down in front of him, and Shep would reach his paw up for a proper introduction. As Billy walked along, he grew more and more sleepy. Shep plopped down across the path, so Billy decided to use him as a pillow.

He leaned up against him and was soon fast asleep.

When Billy woke up, he sat up and looked around. He must not have slept very long as nothing had changed. Everyone was still in their same fishing spots. Billy walked back over to the cousins and climbed out on the tree limb and dangled his feet in the cool water. All he wanted to do was get back to Grandma's. He wondered if Grandma and Jake were ready to go. "Hmmm, let's see, doesn't look like much is going on over there," he thought. Billy yelled, "Hey, Grandma, are you about ready to head back to the house?" Grandma said, "Just give us a few more minutes, Billy. We have to be heading home pretty soon, I'm gonna have to get supper started."

Apparently Billy had been asleep longer than he thought. Jake walked over to the tree limb and pulled up a stringer full of catfish. Billy said, "Hey, how did you catch all of those?"

Jessie said, "It wasn't hard after Sleeping Beauty and the Beast went to sleep and quit making all that racket."

Billy said, "What are you talking about?"

Jessie replied, "As soon as you went to sleep, we started pulling them in. Wasn't much biting on those minnows, so Jake had us try some worms. Larry caught the big one on his cane pole baited with a grasshopper."

Larry said, "You should have seen the fight he put up, I can't believe you slept through all the commotion. I was just sitting here, and all of a sudden, my bobber went under! I thought my whole pole was going into the water, and I was gonna hang on even if I went skiing across the pond, cause there was no way I was going to let go!"

By this time Jessie had already gone to the truck without carrying a thing, and he was laying on the horn nonstop. He just kept honking and honking.

Billy thought, *Why does he always have to cause so much trouble?*

Grandma said, "That kid is gonna run down the battery."

Jake said, "You boys better start loading up all this stuff so we can get back and get these fish cleaned for supper."

Oh boy, Billy thought, *catfish for supper tonight!* They all grabbed a handful of fishing gear and picnic supplies and headed around the pond and through the weeds back to the road where the truck was parked. Jake put one foot on the bottom barbed-wire fence and pulled the other barbed wire up so they could climb through. The horn honking had stopped, much to all their relief. They loaded up the truck, and Larry, Jerry, and Billy sat down on the tail gate for the ride back home. Jake drove slowly and the boys hung their legs down over the tailgate to enjoy the ride. Jake did not realize Jessie was not aboard when he pulled out, or maybe that was the way Jessie had it all planned; Billy wasn't sure. As Jake pulled away, Jessie ran after the truck, trying to jump on the tailgate where all the boys had made room for him to give it a try. Jessie missed, bounced backwards, and hollered out a bad word. Then he made another run at it. Missed again and said another bad word. The boys were all starting to laugh at this point as Jessie took another try. Success at last!

Chapter Twenty-One

Smack Right into Each Other

Billy Bug and Buzz were getting bored waiting for Billy to get back and for the cousins to be gone. They heard the truck coming up the road and could see the trail of dust that followed. *Thank goodness*, they thought. The closer the truck got, the more excited Billy Bug and Buzz became. As the truck pulled off the road, Billy Bug and Buzz could no longer contain themselves. They were both going to fly away at the same time, decided to go the opposite direction, and then smacked right into each other! They laughed at how crazy that must have looked, collected themselves, and flew over by the woodpile to wait and see if they could somehow get to talk with Billy.

Billy, Larry, and Jerry hopped off the tailgate and Jessie jumped over the side of the truck. Jake said, "Come on, boys, let's get these fish cleaned."

Grandma went on into the house to start peeling the potatoes. The boys all gathered around the old worktable in the shade of an old hickory tree with Jake and began to clean the fish. Cleaning fish always seemed pretty awful to Billy, but he always liked to watch, and once they got started, it was not that bad. Jake threw all the cleaned fish in a bowl of water and took it inside for Grandma to fry. The boys could smell the fish and potatoes frying, and they were getting hungrier by the second.

Billy said, "Come on, you guys, let's go get cleaned up and set the table."

They all filed in, and Grandma said, "You boys get cleaned up and get the table set."

Billy said, "Oh Grandma, we know. We're already on the way, we're about to starve to death."

Jake and Jessie were still outside cleaning up the last of the fish-cleaning mess.

Billy Bug and Buzz had quietly watched the fish cleaning.

Billy Bug said, "Buzz, can you believe people eat fish?"

Buzz said, "Billy Bug, can you believe it? How could they?" They heard the screen door slam, and there was Billy. They could hardly contain themselves. Once again, *smack*, they flew right into each other.

"Buzz!" Billy Bug yelled, "You had better stay out of my way."

Buzz said, "Now wait a minute, I think you are always the one in my way!"

Billy threw out the fish-cleaning water and was heading back inside when Billy Bug caught up to him.

"Hey, Billy, what took you so long? Where have you been?" asked Billy Bug.

Billy said, "Billy Bug, it sure is good to see ya, sorry it has been so long, but you guys gotta get out of here before someone sees you."

Billy Bug said, "Oh, Billy, no one is gonna see us. When are we going to get to go see Awryn?"

Billy said, "It won't be long now, the cousins are leaving in the morning. As soon as they leave, I'll meet you guys by the old tractor. You remember where we had the picnic, right?"

"Yeah, we remember," Billy Bug said.

"OK, I'll see you then, but for now you guys need to stay clear of the house. It is too dangerous for you when the cousins are around," said Billy. The screen door slammed. Billy spun around; it was Jessie.

Jessie said, "Hey, Billy, what are you doing over there, talking to yourself?"

Billy answered, "Jessie, why don't you mind your own business?"

Jessie said, "You mind your own business, and come on, Grandma said to tell ya supper's ready."

Billy went in and washed up. By the time he got to the table, everyone was already in their places ready to eat. As soon as supper was over, Billy and the cousins helped clear the table and did the dishes. He had just finished putting the dishes away when Jessie came up with this big idea that would change *everything.* Jessie said, "Come on, you guys, let's go outside and mess around before bedtime."

Larry said, "Yeah, let's go out on the road and catch some toads."

Jessie said, "I got a better idea, I saw some lightning bugs, let's catch 'em!"

Jerry said, "Yeah, let's catch some lightning bugs, I'll get us some jars to put them in!"

Billy was horrified; he said, "No, you guys, I would rather catch some toads. It's more fun to catch toads!"

Jessie said, "No way. I'm going to catch those lightning bugs."

Billy could not do a thing but follow the other boys outside and hope Billy Bug and Buzz were long gone. Then they saw them.

Billy Bug was just about to leave when they heard the screen door slam and saw all the boys coming out. "Look!" Jerry yelled. "There they are!" The boys were charging up to them fast.

Billy Bug said, "Come on, Buzz, we have to get out of here quick!"

Buzz said, "Quick!"

"I told you to come on. Now look, it is too late. Go!" Billy Bug said.

As Jessie swooped up his jar and caught Buzz, Billy Bug darted to the right and smacked right into the back of Larry's jar. Larry slammed the lid on. Billy was stunned in disbelief!

"Got 'em!" Jessie exclaimed. Larry hollered, "Me too, look at mine!" Billy said, "Come on, you guys, let them go."

Jessie said, "Let them go! Are you crazy?"

Larry said, "Come on, Jessie, let's put them on the porch. Hey, do you think lightning bugs would make good fish bait?"

Billy's mind was racing, then he said, "Yeah, I've heard they make the best fish bait there ever was." He was thinking that would give him a chance to let Billy Bug and Buzz go.

Jessie said, "Well, it is too late for that, you know we are leaving first thing in the morning." Then he said, "Come on, Larry, let's take them out and squeeze the lightning juice out of them."

How much could Billy stand? He felt like he was about to lose his mind, and his heart was racing. Billy Bug pressed up against the glass looking for a way to escape. Buzz just sat down at the bottom of the jar and cried and cried; how were they ever going to get out of this one?

Billy finally started to come to his senses and said, "OK, yeah, here—hand over the jars, and I will get them out for you."

Larry said, "Yeah, give Billy the jars, then he can hand us each a lightning bug and we can squeeze the lightning bug juice out of 'em both at the same time."

Jessie and Larry both held out the jars to Billy. Billy had both of his hands full, but at least for the moment he had Billy Bug and Buzz. Billy Bug was flying in circles, and Buzz saw that Billy had them and started jumping up and down like he was on a spring. Billy tucked Buzz's jar under his arm and acted like he was going to unscrew the lid that held Billy Bug in the other jar. Jessie, Larry, and Jerry watched with great anticipation.

Chapter Twenty-Two

Scared and Shaking All Over

Billy backed up, spun quickly to his left, and sprinted towards the road. Jessie, Larry, and Jerry ran after Billy. What was he doing?

"Hey, you get back here!" Larry yelled.

Billy was running as fast as he could down the middle of the dirt road. The dirt was cool on his bare feet. He got the lid to Billy Bug's jar off and let it drop. Billy Bug flew out—free at last! He took a big gulp of the evening air. Billy dropped the empty jar and grabbed Buzz's jar from under his arm. He spun the lid off the top of the jar just as he felt one of the boys grab him from behind and push him forward. Billy felt himself falling; Buzz was scared and was not flying out. Billy Bug had not flown very far away yet, but he was high enough the cousins couldn't reach him. He flew just above them, careful to stay out of reach. Billy hit the dirt and the jar flew out of his hand and landed a few feet in front of him. Larry grabbed it and put his hand over the mouth of the jar. Billy grabbed for Larry and knocked him off balance. Larry lost his grasp of the jar just long enough for Buzz to fly out.

Buzz flew straight up, and he had never flown faster! He was scared and shaking all over. Billy Bug flew over to him and said, "Come on, Buzz, let's get out of here!" Billy Bug and Buzz flew out of sight as fast as they could go and never looked back. Larry and the other boys watched them go.

Jessie said, "Billy, you knucklehead sandwich, what did you do that for? Are you crazy or something? I think you must have lost your pea brain."

Larry said, "Come on, Billy, we were just trying to have a little fun. Now, I'm going to squeeze the bug juice out of you!"

Jerry stuck his hand out to help Billy up, "Come on, you guys, and leave him alone. Let's go back to the house, we're gonna be leaving early in the morning, and I'm pooped."

Billy was so relieved that Billy Bug and Buzz were safe and the cousins would be leaving in the morning. He thought they would never leave.

They all headed toward the house. Jessie said, "We ought to sleep in the basement, it will be cool down there."

Billy had had enough of the cousins and their pranks and scary stories. He said, "You guys sleep wherever you want, I am sleeping in my bed."

Jessie said, "Billy, you're a big chicken." Larry and Jerry both made chicken sounds in unison. "Cluck, cluck, cluck."

Billy said, "I don't care what you guys think, I'm tired of messing with ya." They went into the kitchen. Billy said, "Grandma, can we have a midnight snack before we go to bed?"

"Oh, I suppose, how about some QCM and some cookies?" Mmm, mmm, QCM was always the boys' favorite. It was chocolate granules in a jar that you mixed with milk.

They all filled their glasses and sat down at the table. Grandma got the cookie jar out of the china cabinet. They ate their cookies and drank their QCM in some silence. Billy was glad for it. He was tired, ready to go to bed and get this visit with the cousins behind him.

Jerry said, "I'm ready to go to bed, how about I sleep in your room tonight, Billy?"

Great, thought Billy.

Jessie said, "What? I thought we were gonna sleep down in the basement?"

"Y'all go ahead," Jerry said, "I'm going to stay up here and sleep in Billy's room."

Jessie and Larry picked up their glasses, placed them in the sink, and headed down into the basement. The stairs squeaked, and you could hear each of their steps all the way down.

Billy and Jerry picked up their glasses and took them to the kitchen. Grandma said, "Well, Jerry, guess this is your last night with us for a while. It sure has been good to have all you boys over for a few days. I know Billy always enjoys the company."

Billy said, "Oh, Grandma, I'm going to bed. I'll see you in the morning." Billy and Jerry went to Billy's room. Billy could hear Grandma getting ready for bed in the next room.

Jerry said, "Hey, Billy, let's go and watch Grandma take her hair down." Grandma had her nightgown on and was taking the hairpins out of her hair. She always wore it twisted up on top of her head. When her hair was free from the pins, it tumbled down and almost reached her knees. She brushed it while the boys watched.

She saw the boy's reflections in the mirror and said, "You boys go hop in the bed, and I'll be in to hear you say your prayers."

Billy and Jerry ran to the bedroom and hopped in the bed. Jerry was on the inside, by the wall, and Billy on the outside by the window. He liked to sleep by the window; it was always open wide this time of the year. The night air was cool and clean and smelled so good that Billy always wanted to take big breaths of it. There was a fan on the dresser that rotated back and forth. Billy liked to sing into it sometimes whenever no one was around. He made up all his own songs, just whatever popped in his head. He thought he sounded great. There was an old creepy-looking picture on the wall of Grandma's mom and dad looking very serious. Sometimes the shadows in the room would scare Billy. He often let his imagination run away with him, and he was more than a little afraid of the dark.

Chapter Twenty-Three

Jerry Is Not So Bad

Grandma came in and the boys said their prayers. Grandma told them good night and left the room. "Night," Billy and Jerry said at exactly the same time.

After she left the room, Jerry said, "Hey, Billy, what do you think Larry and Jessie are doing down in the basement?"

Billy said, "Probably trying to scare the wits out of each other. I'm just glad to be in my own bed."

Jerry said, "Me too, Billy, thanks for letting me sleep in here with you."

"Aw, that's OK, Jerry," said Billy. Billy began to think Jerry wasn't so bad after all. "Let's get some sleep. I want to get up early in the morning," he said. Billy had a lot to do with Billy Bug and Buzz. He could hardly wait to see Uncle Luke pull away with all the cousins piled in the truck. Now if he could just get to sleep.

Chapter Twenty-Four

Foreclosure on the Farm

The next morning, Billy woke to the rooster crowing. The sun was just coming up. Billy looked out of the open window; the sky was pink to the east, and the grass was glistening with dew. He could smell bacon cooking. He hopped out of bed and was feeling great; the day for the cousins to leave had finally arrived. Billy went into the kitchen where Grandma was cooking breakfast and Jake was sitting at the table drinking coffee. Billy went to the cabinet to get a cup and sat down at the table. He added his usual two tablespoons of sugar and milk.

Jake said, "How about you and the boys come with me this morning and help me feed the cows?"

Billy said, "I guess we can, but as soon as we get back they're going to have to get ready to go." Billy could not wait for Uncle Luke to get there.

After breakfast was over and the dishes were done, the boys all got in the truck to drive down the hill and feed the cows. Jake pulled around the house slowly and headed down the hill towards the pasture gate. Billy hopped out and got the gate, and Jake pulled the truck through.

"Here come the cows!" Jessie said. Sure enough, here they all came, walking up to get the hay. The boys were throwing out squares of hay from the bales of sweet-smelling alfalfa from the back of the truck.

Jake said, "Billy, go ahead and start counting them while the boys finish up with the hay." Billy liked to count the cows, but it sure was easy to get mixed up because they were always moving around. They had to be counted every morning to make sure none were missing.

Jake and the boys finished feeding and counting the cows and were just getting back to the house, just as Uncle Luke's rickety truck could be heard coming down the road. The truck rolled to a stop. A cloud of dust caught up to it and whooshed over the truck, bumper to bumper. Uncle Luke got out and waved his arm in front of him, trying to clear the air.

"Hello, boys, hello, Jake," Luke said, without much enthusiasm.

Billy said, "Hey, Uncle Luke, boy am I glad to see you!"

Luke said, "Well that's a first. You must be ready for me to get your cousins out of your hair." Luke always thought it was kind of strange for Billy to like to stay at his Grandma's without ever having someone his own age around.

Jake said, "So what'cha been doin', Luke?"

"Oh, working hard, you know me—always something going on." Everyone knew Luke made a point of having as little as possible going on at all times. Luke said, "Bart stopped by to see me the other day. Let's go in and talk for a little bit. You boys get your stuff packed in the truck, I've just got a minute before we head back to town."

Jake and Luke walked up the porch steps and into the kitchen. Grandma was mopping the kitchen floor. She looked up and said, "Hello, Luke, you look worried, what is on your mind?"

Luke said, "Bart came by the other day and said the bank is going to have to foreclose on the farm. Now you have got to come to your senses and realize the time has come. When they auction off everything, you should have enough to get a small place in town."

Grandma looked at Jake, turned to Luke, and said, "You know, Luke, I am not ready to give up the farm. I know Bart gets in a hurry sometimes, but we are going to get the cotton in soon and will be able to give Bart some of the money we owe."

Luke said, "You don't understand, the time is up. Bart is putting the auction together now, they are going to be out here next weekend and sell it all."

Jake had had enough. "OK, Luke, I think we get the picture. I think maybe you should get the boys and head on back to town."

Luke took offense. Who did Jake think he was? Why, he was just the hired hand after all. At least Luke was smart enough not to cross Jake. Luke looked at his mother and said, "I'm heading back to town, I'll see you next weekend, and Bart will be with me. You can expect a crowd."

Grandma said, "You come back with whomever you want, but don't think I'm just going to let them come out here and try to sell this farm out from under me!"

Chapter Twenty-Five

You Have to Be Very Brave Now

Luke stepped off the porch and let the screen door slam behind him. "You boys got all your stuff, let's go." All the boys were unusually quiet; everyone could tell there was something going on and it was not good. The boys said their good-byes, and before Billy knew it, the old truck was pulling back onto the dirt road and was heading back to town. Larry and Jerry were sitting in the back waving good-bye. Billy held his hand up. Billy knew something bad was happening, and he did not have much time.

Grandma and Jake were both still on the porch after seeing the cousins and Luke off. Billy said, "Grandma, I'm going to go exploring."

Grandma was distracted after talking to Jake and said, "Yeah, Billy, that will be fine. Just be back before lunch."

At last Billy was free to do as he pleased. He headed down the hill to try and find Billy Bug and Buzz. When he reached the bottom of the hill, he stopped at the old tractor and was wondering if he would ever see Billy Bug and Buzz again after Larry and Jerry had caught and almost tortured them. *They probably think I'm just like they are,* Billy thought.

Billy was about to wipe the morning dew off the old tractor seat when he heard Billy Bug say, "Billy! There you are. I cannot believe it!" Then he looked worried and said, "Where are those cousins of yours?"

Billy said, "Don't worry, Billy Bug, they finally left. Where is Buzz, has he recovered from being caught?"

Billy Bug said, "Are you kidding? He won't shut up about it! His story gets better every time he tells it. The last I heard he was saying what a hero he was and that it was a good thing he did not scare easily. You and I had completely lost our wits. According to Buzz, if it weren't for him, there would have been no way we could have gotten out of there with our 'bug juice.'"

Billy laughed and said, "I am just glad you both lived to tell the tale. I was so afraid they were going to mash both of you."

"They would have too if it were not for you, Billy. You know, you saved both of our lives. Everyone else knows it too, regardless of Buzz's version," Billy Bug said.

Billy said, "You know, Billy Bug, things are really getting bad at Grandma's. When Luke came to pick up the cousins, I heard him telling Grandma that Bart from the bank was going to come out and auction everything off next weekend, and she would have to move to town. Billy Bug, there is no way that can happen. Grandma would not know what to do living in town. What about Jake? The farm is all he knows. It just isn't fair."

Billy Bug said, "Well, we better get going, it doesn't sound like we have much time left. Thank goodness those cousins of yours have finally gone home where they belong! What a pain in the lightning rear they were! Let's go to the tree and see Awryn."

Billy thought, "Oh boy, here we go again." He still didn't quite know what to think of everything that was going on. *I used to just go exploring and hang out with Grandma and Jake,* he thought. "Now I go around talking to lightning bugs and fairies whenever I get the chance. I like Awryn and all, but she is a girl after all!" They made their way across the field and stopped outside of the tree. Billy said, "Oh shoot, Billy Bug! I don't have my flashlight! Now what am I going to do?"

Billy Bug said, "Aw, come on, Billy, just follow me! I'll light the way." Billy spread the branches apart to squeeze through. They went through the opening together; Billy Bug flew a little ahead and lit the way.

It took a few seconds for Billy's eyes to adjust to the light, which was very dim with only Billy Bug to light the way. Billy could see the beautiful colors on the walls that sparkled with all the magic they contained. On the floor of the old tree was a worn path that led to the lake. Billy knew the turn was right up ahead. If he could just manage to stay close enough to Billy Bug to see the way. At last they made it to the big room. The lake seemed even bigger than last time. The entire area was alive with movement. The frogs jumped, butterflies flew over the flowers, and all around the shore, there were dragonflies everywhere. The entire area was awash in the light from the fairy dust that reflected off the lake in all the colors of the rainbow.

Finally, Billy saw Awryn sitting on what appeared to be a rock right by the water's edge. As he got closer, he saw that it was not a rock it all. Awryn was sitting on the biggest turtle Billy had ever seen. The turtle slowly turned and looked at Billy and grinned a toothless grin. Awryn said, "Billy! At last you have returned, what has kept you away for so long? I was beginning to wonder if you would ever come back."

Billy said, "It's a long story, Awryn, I would tell you all of it, but I'm running out of time. Things are getting really bad for Grandma. I don't see what can be done to help save the farm now. There just isn't enough time."

Awryn said, "I've been thinking, Billy, and there is only one thing to do. Come with me, we have to go see my father, King Augustus, king of all the fairies. He is very wise and he will know what to do."

Billy said, "Oh, I don't know, Awryn." He was more than a little afraid to meet Awryn's father, especially now knowing he was the Fairy King.

Billy Bug flew over to Billy and said, "Gee, Awryn, I don't know if that is such a good idea. I have heard your father is very powerful. I don't think he is going to want to be bothered. What if he is angry that Billy is even here in this secret place? He might think Billy will tell the others, and then what would happen to all the fairies?"

Awryn said, "Now, now. Don't be afraid, I have already spoken to Father, and I have to admit he was very angry at first, but I think he has calmed down enough at least to see Billy." She said, "Billy, you have to be very brave now. There is nothing else left to do. We are out of time."

Billy said, "That may be, but what am I going to say to the King of all Fairies? Why should he help somebody like me?"

Awryn said, "He is a great king, and he will help. He is good and kind, he is just a little scary at first."

Chapter Twenty-Six

A Tree That Needs Protection

Awryn stood up, and the big turtle slowly slid out into the water. She said, "OK, you two just follow me." With that she stepped out into the water. Well, not really the water but where the water should have been. Suddenly, there was a big rushing sound like all the water was being sucked down, and a huge castle began to rise from the water with a staircase bigger than Billy could have ever imagined. Awryn walked where the water once was and led Billy and Billy Bug up the staircase. At the very top, there was a great door that slowly swung open. Billy was more afraid than he had ever been. *How could any of this be happening?* he thought.

Awryn said, "Come on now, guys, it is too late to turn back now." They stepped through the door side by side, and there he was! Sitting on a huge throne was King Augustus, King of all the Fairies. When he spoke, his voice was very deep, and the air in the room seemed to disappear. Billy's heart was pounding; he was afraid it was going to explode. Billy Bug dived to the bottom of Billy's shirt pocket. He was trembling and could not get control of his fear; his mind was racing faster than Billy's heart. King Augustus said, "Hello, Billy, Awryn has told me about you and, shall we say, your little problem?"

Hoping and praying all that was good and all the strength and wisdom of his ancestors before him was with him now, Billy mustered every ounce of courage he had. He stepped forward and looked up into the face of the mighty Fairy King. He said, "Yes, sir, my Grandma and I do have a problem. It is a very big problem. You see, sir, our whole lives and everything we hold dear is at stake." Billy was amazed his voice was shaking but actually working.

King Augustus looked at Billy. "I realize the gravity of your situation, and you see, you are not in this alone. Our entire kingdom is under the canopy of one of your grandmother's trees. A tree that needs protection and that cannot withstand a change. What would happen if someone bought your grandmother's farm and decided to cut down all the trees? Our kingdom would be scattered to the four winds—north, east, south, and the west. However, if I gather all my armies to try and assist, I would be risking exposure of the fairy kingdom and endangering all that I hold dear and have ever known. After much consideration, I have decided I will help you, Billy. As you can see, we are somewhat in the same situation. If I choose to sit idly by and not help, I too would be putting the kingdom in jeopardy. I choose to take the risk and fight for what is good and what is right."

Billy felt a wave of relief come over him. Somehow he felt like King Augustus *could* help! "Thank you, Your Majesty!" is all he could think to say.

Awryn stepped forward and said, "Thank you, Father."

Augustus said, "At nightfall I will send all my legions into the cotton fields."

Billy thought, *In the cotton fields? What could they possibly do there?* He said, "I don't understand."

King Augustus said, "I will need your help. Come to the cotton field when the full moon rises. We will work by the moonlight, the cotton will grow and be harvested this very night. Sell that cotton, Billy, and the farm will be saved."

Billy said, "I do not understand, sir. The cotton is not ready to be picked, how can it grow and be picked all in one night?"

Augustus said, "You do not need to understand. That is all."

Billy said, "But—"

Awryn quickly grabbed his arm and whispered, "Please, Billy, let's go, and we must never ever doubt my father."

Billy's mind was racing. He was confused and wondered how the king's plan could possibly work. There was so much to do, and hadn't he heard Jake say the cotton would not be ready to pick for three weeks? They walked out of the castle where there was a wooden boat with huge sails, carvings, and scrolls at each end waiting for them, as the lake had now come up and surrounded the castle. When the boat got them back to shore, Billy looked back, and the castle was once again invisible to him. All of a sudden, Buzz flew up and said, "Hey, Billy! It's about time you got back. Where is Billy Bug? Hiding out somewhere, I suppose."

Billy Bug peeked out of Billy's shirt pocket and said, "Shows what you know about it. I'd say it is about time *you* showed back up. Come on, we've got work to do."

Buzz said, "Oh, now I guess you think you are the boss of me, Mr. High and Mighty."

Irritated, Billy Bug said, "Now listen, Buzz, I have had just about enough of you! We have been to see King Augustus, and he is going to help us save the farm tonight!"

Buzz said, "Yeah right, sure you have."

Billy Bug said, "Buzz, you're wearing me out. I don't have time to explain it all. If you were not off telling your wild versions of stories, you would have been with us instead of wondering what is going on now."

Billy said, "What do you think will happen tonight Awryn?"

"I do not know," she replied, "but if Father is sending out the whole army, it is going to be big. Hurry, Billy, the sun is going down."

They made their way back to the entrance to the tree, and Billy squeezed through the crack once again. Billy Bug and Buzz flew to the lead, and Awryn lagged behind. Billy said, "You are coming with us, right, Awryn?"

"Oh sure, of course I am. It just seems so strange to leave the canopy especially not knowing what this night will bring." She had never seen her father's entire army mobilized before.

Billy said, "Let's head on over to the cotton field." The full moon was just coming up. Billy thought, *Gramaw has got to be worried. He should have been back hours ago.* He hated to think of making Gramaw worry about him when she already was so worried about the farm. But if the king's plan worked, surely she will be feeling better soon. Billy's mind was racing.

Billy Bug said, "We can light the way for you, and it is not like Awryn needs any help." Indeed, Awryn had already raced ahead and was flying back towards them with a trail of glowing fairy dust in all shades of pink, green, and blue sparkling behind her.

Chapter Twenty-Seven

Sarge Leading the Charge

Billy heard a trumpet in the not-so-far-off distance. Then he saw them coming! It was the army. Legions of dragonflies with fairies carrying bags of fairy dust riding on their backs. Sarge was leading the charge with King Augustus riding on his back. Sarge had a very determined look on his face, and the king had a great staff that he was pointing directly at the cotton field.

Billy looked up in amazement. The army brigade was so large that when they passed over Billy and the others, they blocked the stars from view. "*Wow!* What in the world do you think they are going to do? Where did they all come from?" asked Billy.

Awryn answered, "Oh, they have always been here, you have just never seen them all at the same time."

Billy started running towards the cotton field. He ran down one of the ruts in the road made by the pickup when Jake drove down to the pasture to feed and count the cows. He was running as fast as he could, and the army was still swarming overhead; it seemed to never end. Billy Bug, Buzz, and Awryn flew just far enough ahead for Billy to keep up. Billy was already tiring from the long run but could see the cotton field. This gave him the stamina he needed to continue to run. The cool, damp night air cooled his burning lungs. The army was now flying low over the field; King Augustus gave the signal for the army to stop, and the army now hovered over the entire cotton field. He pointed his staff up in the air and waved it in a circular motion. The fairy riders simultaneously began to empty the contents of their bags. The night sky and the cotton field turned beautiful colors; the full moon was reflecting the various shades of fairy dust. The dust settled onto the cotton field and began to glow.

Suddenly the earth below the cotton field began to rumble; Billy began to stumble and tried to stay upright. The cotton plants started to sway and shake and grow! Then one began to pop and then another until the entire field was popping cotton balls! *Pop, pop, pop,* the cotton balls began to pile up higher and higher. Billy stood at the edge of the field and began to laugh, and then he ran into the field and began to throw cotton balls into the air. The army stayed in formation above the field. The cotton was beginning to make quite a heap now; it was as far as Billy could see. The cotton was almost up to Billy's chest!

Awryn flew down and said, "Billy, please back up before you are buried in cotton." At that point, Billy thought that sounded like a pretty good idea!

He struggled back to the edge of the growing mound of cotton. His mind was racing with questions and possibilities. Surely with all this cotton the farm would be saved. This would also protect the fairy kingdom. The cotton continued to pop and formed a great white mountain.

The sun would be coming up soon. The horizon was beginning to glow with the pinkness of the coming day. The army began to descend in a great circular formation around the mountain of cotton. King Augustus, riding upon Sarge's back, came into view. Sarge hovered just above Billy's head, and the king spoke directly to Billy. Billy Bug and Buzz's legs were shaking. They were not used to being in such a close proximity to the king, and it made them very nervous. The king said, "Billy, we have done as you have requested, there is a great fortune of cotton here, surely more than is needed. Now we will need your help. We do not travel far from the fairy kingdom and know little of human ways."

Billy said, "I don't understand, how I can help?"

"We will need you to show us where to take the cotton from here," said King Augustus. "I can do that!" Billy exclaimed with relief. *Thank goodness I could be of help after the fairies have done so much!* he thought. "All we need to do is get the cotton to the mill. It is almost daylight, the sun has already begun to come up, and very soon there will be people out starting their day. How can we get to the mill with all this cotton without being seen?" said Billy.

"Billy, we can move the cotton to where it needs to go, but you must lead the way," said the king.

"But it would take me all day to walk all the way to the mill!" said Billy nervously. His mind was reeling. He didn't want to endanger his friends.

Chapter Twenty-Eight

The Great White Cloud

King Augustus pointed his great staff towards the pink sky, and in the far distance, Billy could see a winged horse. The horse was magnificent. It was as white as snow and had wings that spanned across its back. The horse flew to the fairy king and stopped near Billy, so close that he could see his black eyes that were as big as silver dollars. Then the king spoke once more to Billy; he said, "Billy, this is Lassiter, we have been friends since the earth was new. I want you to ride him and show us the way to the mill." Billy's mind was once again a whirl with questions.

For starters, he thought, how am I going to get on such a giant horse, and how is a mountain of cotton even going to be moved? Billy was afraid he had gotten everyone involved in something he could not control. Lassiter came very close to Billy, and he could see all the muscles under his white coat. The horse then knelt down on his front knees, and Billy took hold of his long white mane and swung his leg over, and before he knew it, he was astride the magnificent creature. He was aboard the great white winged horse! Lassiter reared his front legs into the air and leaped into the sky. Billy Bug and Buzz raced into Billy's shirt pocket; they were not going to miss out on this. Awryn sat on one of Lassiter's wings and looked over and gave Billy a big smile, as if she were having the time of her life!

Sarge brought the king over to speak further with Billy. He said, "OK, Billy, now all you have to do is to lead the way. We are all counting on you."

Billy's heart was racing! He nudged Lassiter towards town and the cotton mill. The horse flew higher than Billy was expecting. He looked down, and everything looked small and the clouds seemed very close. Billy looked back. The great mountain of cotton was lifting off the ground. The army was underneath, lifting it higher and higher. Soon it was so high off the ground it looked like a great white cloud moving across the morning sky.

Billy Bug and Buzz poked their heads over the edge of Billy's shirt pocket, and their antennae's blew back in the breeze. Billy Bug looked at Buzz and said, "I cannot wait to hear all the stories that you will tell about last night, and now this! Can you believe it?"

Buzz said, "Oh yeah, I can believe it, I knew it all along."

"Oh really, I guess you and the old king worked it out amongst yourselves?" said Billy Bug.

"Now, now, there you go getting all in a huff again. I am just saying I was thinking about it and what the plan might be," Buzz replied.

Billy was beginning to get worried. The sun was getting higher by the minute, and they still had quite a way to go to reach town and the cotton mill.

Awryn said, "Do not worry, Billy, everything is going to work out, just wait and see." They flew on a little further and she said, "Look, I think I can see the town from here! Is that it?"

Billy nudged Lassiter to begin to fly downward toward the mill. He looked over his shoulder, and the army and the great cloud of cotton were still following close behind. He looked down again and could see Bart the Banker's fancy car with Bart driving and puffing on a fat cigar. Then Billy saw someone else. It was Uncle Luke riding shotgun. *What in the world?* Billy thought. He realized right then they were heading west of town. "They must be going to Grandma's. Oh no, we're too late!" yelled Billy.

Lassiter's hooves were just touching down on the gravel driveway of the mill as the army was setting the mountain of cotton down in the mill parking lot. The giant mountain of cotton was three times as big as the entire mill! Billy knew the cotton crop was gigantic but had no idea how much there really was until he saw it sitting next to the mill. All of a sudden, King Augustus flew over next to Billy and Awryn. He said, "Come, Awryn, we must leave before we are all discovered." Awryn flew to her father and waved good-bye to Billy, Billy Bug, and Buzz.

As Sarge turned to take them back to the fairy tree, she looked back and said, "Good luck, Billy, I hope you will still come to see me." Sarge and the entire army were already almost out of sight as Billy waved good-bye.

Billy slid off Lassiter's back. He could not believe he had ridden on that magnificent horse. Lassiter looked at him with his great black eyes, nodded his head, then reared up and took flight.

Chapter Twenty-Nine

Biscuit Hill Café

Gus the mill worker was just finishing his last cup of coffee at the Biscuit Hill Café. He paid his check and left Wanda the waitress a nickel tip and headed outside to his old dusty pickup. He pressed on the starter, and the engine did not start. He gave it another try, and the old girl started up; he revved the motor just for good measure, put her in gear, and drove up the hill and around the bend. When he rounded the bend and started back down the other side of the hill, he could see the mill. He could not believe his eyes! "Well, cut my legs off and call me Shorty!" he said, when he saw the great mountain of cotton and a boy standing outside waiting for the mill to open.

Billy Bug and Buzz zipped and whirled around Billy's head. Billy said, "Come on, you guys, cut it out! Here comes Gus. Get in my pocket and stay quiet!" Buzz walked on the edge of Billy's pocket as if it were a tightrope; Billy Bug gave him a push and sent him over the edge into the pocket.

Gus pulled his old truck up next to Billy. His mouth was agape as he was staring at the cotton. Finally he said, "Morning, Billy. What in the world are you doing in town by yourself? Did you see who dropped off this load of cotton?"

"Yes sir Gus, it's mine. Well, mine, Grandma's, and Jake's anyway. I need to get paid for it quick, Gus, I just saw Bart and Uncle Luke driving out towards Grandma's place."

"Well, I'll bet you did," Gus said. "This is auction day, Billy, I guess the whole town will be driving out soon. You say this is your cotton?" Gus asked. "How did you get it here, and how in the world did you get to harvest it so soon? Billy, there must still be a good month before the first cotton crops are due!"

Billy said, "Gus, I do not have time to explain it right now, we gotta get paid for this cotton and get out to Grandma's quick. How much do ya think we will get for this much cotton?"

"Well, good gosh, Billy, I'll bet you have enough here to buy the mill if you wanted it!" exclaimed Gus. "Can't tell for sure of course until we weigh it all, but that's gonna take some time, Billy."

"Gus, I do not have time for that, they could be auctioning off the farm right now!"

Gus said, "Now you just calm yourself down. Come on, get in the truck and I'll give you a lift out to your grandma's place." Billy climbed in the truck, and Gus pulled onto the gravel road that headed out of town towards the farm.

"Please hurry, Gus, I can't stand it! What if we are too late?" said Billy in a tiff.

"Now, Billy, you just settle down over there. We'll make it, you'll see," Gus said with a smile.

Chapter Thirty

We Are Too Late!

At last Gus and Billy were within sight of Grandma's house. Billy could see the long line of cars parked on both sides of the road. He looked at Gus and said, "Now Billy, you do not know that, just hold on. You can see for yourself soon enough," Gus said. "I know that auctioneer, and ole Hank—well, he doesn't do anything fast, especially talk!" Gus began honking the old truck's horn as he pulled up and parked as close as he could get. Before he knew it, Billy had already leaped out of the truck seat and was running down the side of the road between the cars.

There were a group of men standing in a semicircle around the porch. Grandma and Jake were on the porch looking out at the crowd. Bart the Banker was also on the porch, speaking to the crowd of men. He was giving directions as to how the auction would proceed and the order of the sale.

"I knew it, I told you Gus,

"First up for bid will be the farmhouse and all the surrounding property. Then we will move on to the truck and trailers, the tractor, and the implements. After all of that has been sold, we'll move to the toolshed, and lastly, all the livestock will be sold," Bart crowed, as he strutted around Grandma's porch like a proud old rooster.

Grandma had tears welling up in her eyes, but she would not cry. No, not now. She must wait to fall apart in private, as she knew she surely would do, but only when the time was right. Not here, not now in front of the crowd, not in front of the heartless banker, Bart. Jake stood proudly by Grandma's side; he would not bow his head or look ashamed. Why should he? He had worked hard every day of his entire life; what could he have possibly done to change what was happening today?

Bart concluded his speech, puffed his chest out importantly, and said, "Now then, gentlemen, if there are not any questions, let's get this auction started. We'll make an early day of it, what do you say? Let's get started, Hank!"

we are too late!"

Hank began, "First off, the house and property will go to the highest bidder." he said. "What's the first bid for this beautiful old farmhouse?" The bidding began, and there were several investors and developers bidding against each other for the beautiful farm.

Billy stood and watched as if he were in a dream. Billy Bug snapped him back to attention. He looked over the edge of Billy's pocket and said, "Hey, Billy! Snap out of it, you have got to do something!"

Billy looked at Grandma, at the auctioneer, and at the crowd. Hank the auctioneer would say some sort of mumbo jumbo Billy did not understand, then holler out a dollar amount, and someone in the crowd would raise their hand. The dollar amount kept getting higher and higher, but the hand-raising began to slow down.

Finally, the amount stayed the same, and the auctioneer said, "Going once, going twice." Billy flung his arm in the air, but he was too small, and the auctioneer could not see it! Billy panicked and raced to the front of the crowd yelling, "Here, here!" He was jumping and waving his arm wildly in the air. At last Hank the auctioneer saw Billy at the same time as the entire crowd, Bart the Banker, and Grandma. Billy looked at Grandma. Apparently it had all become too much for her. She looked very sad; she held her head high, but Billy could see the tear as it spilled over and ran down her cheek.

The auctioneer said, "Now, son, I am sorry, but if you place a bid at an auction, you have to have the money to back it up."

Billy said, "But—"

And the auctioneer turned away from Billy and said, "Now, where were we folks?" Gus had finally made it to Billy's side. He said, "Hey, Hank! Hold on just a ding-dang minute there. This here little fellow does have the money to back up any bid he makes. Why, I'd say he can buy the farm and just about anything else for sale at this auction today if he has a mind to."

Now the crowd roared with laughter! Bart had all he could stand. He strode over to the auctioneer and said, "OK, Hank, now that is enough. I know that this little fellow is staying here with his grandmother, and this is a difficult time for them all. However, the situation is his grandmother is in default on her loan due to the unpaid taxes, and this property is for sale today. Now let's get on with it!"

Gus said, "Bart, I think you better hold on a minute. I am telling you and everyone else the sale has got to stop. Billy has got the money for the taxes in full, there is no need to go any further!"

Bart turned bright red; he was getting madder by the minute.

Gus went on to say, "You should have seen what I saw earlier this morning. I was just coming down the road from the Biscuit Hill, and there it was! The biggest mountain of cotton I ever saw! Why I'm telling you all there is no way the mill can contain it, we are going to have to bale it up and send at least half of it over to Elk City by the truckload."

The crowd was silent and stared in disbelief. *How could it be?* they all wondered. They soon began to murmur to each other.

Bart said, "Gus, I have known you my entire life, but I gotta tell you, I think you have really flipped your lid this time."

Gus said, "Oh yeah, Mr. High and Mighty? You better watch yourself. Remember, I have known you all your life as well. Way before you was Mr. Uppity Up. I'm telling you it's some sort of miracle! Now before you make a big mistake, let's all go to the mill right now if you cannot take my word for it. Let's all go see us a beautiful mountain of cotton. This sale is not going a bit further, I'm telling ya now."

Suddenly the entire crowd began to move. All the farmers and townspeople scrambled to be the first back in town to see what was going on at the mill. When they had made their way to their cars and pickups, Billy was left standing, looking up at Grandma and Jake, who still remained unmoved on the porch. Grandma said, "Billy, what have you done?"

Billy replied, "I hope we have saved the farm, do you think a mountain of cotton is enough?"

Jake said, "Oh yes, Billy. I don't know what's going on yet, but Gus wouldn't stop the sale if he wasn't sure. Billy, you've got to tell us where it came from."

As soon as Billy Bug and Buzz heard Jake say that it would be enough cotton to save the farm, they could no longer contain themselves in Billy's shirt pocket. They banged and bumped off each other until they freed themselves and flew in front of Billy. Billy Bug flew to Billy's ear and whispered, "*Yahoo!* I am going to tell the others!"

Buzz did a backflip and shouted, "*Yahoo!* I am going to beat Billy Bug down to the tree to tell the others!" With that, they both flew out of sight before Billy could say a word.

Now Billy was truly alone with Grandma and Jake, but what could he say? He surely could not tell them. They would never believe it anyway. He stepped off the porch and was looking around, trying to think of what to say. He looked down at the ground and scratched a semicircle line in the sand with his tennis shoe.

Grandma could see Billy's predicament and said, "Now, Jake, I don't see why it really matters where Billy got the cotton. The farm is saved!"

With that, she jumped in the air, put her hand over her mouth in awe, and said, "Can you believe it, Jake? It truly is a miracle!"

Jake grinned, tucked his elbow through hers, and they both kicked up their heels and spun around for a few circles on the front porch. Old Shep got so excited he reared up on his back legs and barked and barked. Finally, Jake collected himself enough to say, "Well, come on. We better hightail it down to the mill and take a look at Billy's mountain of cotton for ourselves!"

Before Billy knew it, they were all in the truck headed to town; Grandma and Jake sat up front, and he and Shep rode in the back. Shep held his head over the side, and the wind blew his ears back, and he looked like he was smiling all the way to town. Billy could not remember ever feeling so good.

Chapter Thirty-One

Seems Like We've Been Waiting on Something Our Whole Lives

Jake steered the truck around the bend in the road and headed down the hill to the cotton mill. Then they saw it—halfway down the hill, Jake stopped the truck right in the middle of the road. He and Grandma just sat there staring with their mouths wide open. Billy watched both of them from the back of the truck. Jake slowly turned and looked at Grandma and said, "Don't that beat all you've ever seen?" Grandma still had not come back to her senses enough to speak. Jake put the truck in gear, and they began to slowly roll down the hill, toward the crowd and the great mountain of cotton. Jake pulled off to the side of the road. They were going to have to get out and walk a ways, as the townspeople's cars and trucks filled what was left of the old Mills parking lot. There were cars and pickups parked all alongside the road.

Billy jumped over the side of the truck bed as Grandma and Jake stepped out of the truck. Jake and Grandma still looked as if they were in a bit of daze. Billy told Shep to stay in the back of the truck and led the way down the side of the road. The grass was still wet with the morning dew, and soon all their shoes were wet with bits of grass and seeds stuck to them. Soon the crowd saw them approaching and started cheering and shouting.

"Can you believe it?" "Hurry up and get over here, can you see it?" "Have you ever seen so much cotton in one place in all your life?" "What is it all about?" "Where did it come from?" Billy heard people saying. It seemed like everyone had a smile and a question. The crowd stepped aside so Grandma, Jake, and Billy could walk through to the base of the cotton mountain. When they got there, Bart the Banker and Uncle Luke were already there. Both had a big smile on their faces. Bart seemed a little too happy. He always made Billy nervous. All Bart could think about was all the money the cotton would bring in that would surely be deposited into his bank. Billy was sure Uncle Luke was already thinking about how he would wiggle-worm his way into the fortune and never have to work another day. Billy thought to himself, *Work another day—I wonder if he ever really worked one whole day in his lazy life.*

Uncle Luke was the first to speak. "Well, Bart, how much do you think it is worth?"

Bart replied, "There is only way to find out. Gus, get on with it. If you don't start getting that cotton weighed, we are never going to figure out how much it is worth now, are we?"

Gus started his work; it was going to take at least a week and who knows how many trucks. He did not like Bart bossing him around like that in front of the whole town. He had grown tired of the crowd and especially Bart. After all, he did have a "mountain" of work in front of him, and he did not need spectators. Gus spoke up directly to the crowd, "OK, show's over. I have work to do, and I can't do it with all you looky-loos standing around in the way. It wouldn't be safe." Then he looked at Grandma and Uncle Jake and motioned them to the side where he could speak privately with them, out of earshot of all the townspeople. "I want you both to know I aim to see you get every single penny that this cotton will bring. It is going to take me at least a week to get it all baled and weighed. As soon as I do, I will come out to the house and let you know what it will bring. I will give you a receipt for it. You take that receipt and deal with Bart or whoever you need to. At that point I am going to be out of it. I have no intention of dealing with Bart, Mr. High and Mighty Banker. I am telling you, I have just about had my fill of him."

Grandma thanked Gus and said, "Well, Jake, I trust Gus, and I know he will do right by us. I guess there is nothing left to do now but wait and see."

Jake said, "Seems like we been waiting on something our whole lives. Waiting on rain, waiting on the crops to grow, waiting to see if they will bring in enough to get us through another year. It's different this time, now we are waiting, but we know it is all going to work out, thanks to Billy that is."

Billy felt his face turning red from the attention; he puffed his chest out and felt at least a half a foot taller. Then he realized it was not really thanks to him, and he had to say so. He said, "I had lots of help from friends. I cannot tell you about them, but please know they are the ones that made it all happen. They helped because they wanted to, because it was the right thing for all of us. I know you both wonder about them, but some things are best not told. Isn't that so, Grandma?"

She replied, "I understand, Billy. Your secret will always be safe with us. But I must ask you one favor, Billy. Please thank them for us. They have saved our home. They may not realize it, our home is not much, but we will always be so very grateful for what they have done."

Billy said, "Oh no, Grandma, they will understand because they know how important home is—they have one too, you know!"

Jake said, "Well, it's best we get going. I am going to stop on the way and take down every one of those auction signs."

Billy said, "Before we go home, can we stop at the store? I surely would like to buy some penny candy. I have a quarter I have been saving. Can we, Jake?"

Jake smiled and said, "No, Billy. You keep on saving that quarter. I have one for you to spend today. After what you have done, I'll be the one buying the candy."

Jake pulled the truck up to the curb. He turned to Billy and said, "You can go ahead and pick it out."

Billy stepped inside the store; Herb was behind the counter and greeted Billy with an ear-to-ear smile. Billy thought, *Boy, Herb has never looked so happy to see me.*

Herb said, "What can I do for you, Billy?"

Billy said, "Aw, I'm just gonna get some candy real quick, Grandma and Jake are waiting outside for me." Billy walked over to the candy aisle and picked up twenty-five pieces of candy and tried to keep from dropping any of it. He managed to get to the counter and placed all the candy on the counter and dug in his pocket for the quarter and placed it on the counter. He placed his finger on the edge of the quarter and slid it towards Herb.

Herb did the same and slid the quarter back to Billy. He said, "Billy, this candy is on the house today. I heard what you did for your Grandma and the farm."

Billy was shocked; he took the bag of candy and said, "Gee, thanks, Herb." Billy headed for the door and looked back, and there was Herb, still smiling. Billy thought about what a good a day it had been.

When Billy got back in the truck, he handed the quarter back to Jake and said, "Herb wouldn't take it."

Jake looked at Billy and said, "Well, I'll be darned, I never knew Herb to give anything away." All the way home, Jake pulled over at every auction sign, got out, pulled up the sign, and threw them all in the back of the truck.

Grandma was being awfully quiet, but she mostly just seemed relieved. When they turned on to the dirt road, Billy saw a car pulled off the side of the road by the house. Grandma said, "Well look, Billy, your mom is here!"

"Surely summer can't be over so soon." Billy thought his heart was racing. He was so mixed up. He was always ready to see his mother, and he always missed her badly during the summers at Grandma's. This time it was different. How could he leave Billy Bug and Buzz? Then he thought about Awryn and the fairy kingdom.

Chapter Thirty-Two

Slow It Down to About 95

Jake parked the truck, and Billy was suddenly very excited to see his mom. He hurried into the house and found her in the guest room. She was just starting to unpack her things. She heard Billy come in and ran over and scooped him up in her arms. Well, as much as she could. Billy was getting so big. As she looked at Billy, tears started to well up in her eyes. Billy felt the same way; he was so glad to see her. "Oh, Billy," she said, "I have missed you soooo much. It has seemed like such a long summer this year. Tell me everything, Billy—did you have a good time? Are you ready to go back to the city?"

There was so much to tell Billy did not know where to start. He said, "Mom, I have been so busy, I've not even thought about going home, I haven't even gotten homesick like I usually do. I have got all kinds of good stuff to tell you, but it is going to take a while, and I am busy right now."

"Busy?" Billy's mom said. "How can you be so busy when I just got here? All I want to do is spend time with you and hear all the stories about your summer!"

Grandma made it into the house and saw Ellen. She gave her a great big hug and said, "Oh, Ellen, it is so good to see you. You will not believe what all has been going on here on the farm! Ellen, Billy has saved the farm from the bank!"

Ellen looked confused, and then she looked at Billy. Billy thought, *Oh boy, this is going to take a while, and I have got to get down to the tree to let Awryn know everything is going to be OK.*

Grandma could see Billy's dismay and said, "Come into the kitchen, Ellen, and I will make us some lemonade and I'll tell you all about it. Go ahead and play for a while," she said to Billy, and gave him a wink. Billy's smile lit up the room. He gave his mom another big hug and said, "I won't be long." He turned and ran for the door and almost knocked Jake over on his way out.

Jake said, "Hey, slow it down to about ninety-five, little fella, is the house on fire?"

Billy called back over his shoulder, "No, but my tennis shoes are going be, from me running so fast."

Jake just smiled, took his hat off, and rubbed his head as he shook it.

When Shep saw Billy run by so fast, it gave him such a start he decided to get up and run along after him to see what all the commotion was about. Mind you, this is something he did not do much these days; he would just as soon lie around in the shade. Why, he would hardly get up to chase a jack rabbit anymore. He followed Billy at a fast trot. This was as much as he could muster. Billy ran down the hill so fast he almost lost control of himself and thought he was going to fall forward and go head over heels the rest of the way. He finally reached the bottom of the hill and kept right on running. "Oh no!" shouted Billy. "The candy!" He quickly turned and ran back up the hill. He passed Shep coming down the hill and that was *it*. Shep thought, *OK, that does it. I knew I should not have gotten up to run after him.* Shep headed for the closest shady spot about halfway down the hill and plopped down.

Billy Bug and Buzz had been hanging around the old tractor and saw Billy running down the hill. Right before he got to them, he suddenly turned and started back the other way. Billy Bug said, "See, Buzz, he took one look at you and ran the other direction."

Buzz said, "I think you got it backwards. Billy is always glad to see me. You, on the other hand, have got to be getting on his nerves by now. Why, you are about to wear me out and I *have* to put up with you!"

Billy Bug said, "Buzz, why are you always trying to start something with me?"

Buzz said, "Oh no. There you go again. I am not *starting* anything with you, I am trying to *finish* something."

Billy Bug had all he could stand and was just about to fly as far as he could get from "Bothersome" Buzz when he saw Billy running back down the hill. Shep just barked when he went by—sure beat getting up again.

Billy was running so fast he did not see Billy Bug and Buzz sitting on the tractor; he ran right by them. Billy Bug said, "Come on, Buzz, let's catch him!"

Buzz said, "There you go again, always in my business. Telling me what to do like you are the boss of me."

Billy Bug did not bother to respond; he had already caught up to Billy. He said, "Hey, Billy, what's the big hurry?"

Billy stopped and said, "Boy am I glad to see you!" just as Buzz caught up to them.

Buzz said, "Well then, you must be beside yourself at the sight of me!"

Billy Bug said, "Ignore him, Billy, he has been at it all day."

Buzz said, "Ignore me! Who could ignore me—I am a force of nature."

"A freak of nature is more like it!" said Billy Bug.

"It is great to see both of you," Billy said. "We did it! We saved Grandma's farm!"

Billy Bug and Buzz started buzzing around and around. They were so happy they did not know what to do with themselves.

Billy said, "Come on, you two, I was just heading to the tree. I want to tell Awryn and the whole fairy kingdom!" Billy ran toward the tree. When he got there, he was so out of breath he could barely speak.

Awryn was sitting on one of the branches at the top of the tree and could see them coming. She said, "Billy! I was wondering if I would ever see you again."

Billy looked at her in disbelief; how could she think she would never see him again? Billy tried to catch his breath and managed to say, "Why would you say something like that, after all you have done?"

She said, "Oh, Billy, what is all the huffing and puffing about? I saw you from the top of the hill, you have been running around like you have lost your mind."

Billy managed to blurt out, "We did it, Awryn, we did it!"

Buzz said, "Yeah, we did it! We did it!" He suddenly did a somersault in midair.

Awryn asked, "So it worked? It really worked? The entire kingdom has been talking about it."

"Yes," Billy said. "It worked! Jake pulled all the auction signs up on the way home from the mill. Our homes are saved!"

Chapter Thirty-Three

Heroes Are Grown-Ups

Now Awryn was as excited as everyone else as she flew down to Billy. "Come on, Billy, we've got to tell the others!" Awryn led the way inside the tree; Billy Bug and Buzz had landed on Billy's shoulder. Every time Billy went inside the tree, he was just as amazed as that first time, when Billy Bug had been with him to help light the way. Billy left his footprints in the fairy dust, while the others always left it undisturbed. They turned the bend and entered into the great room. The lake was calm, as smooth as glass. Billy thought it looked as though you could walk on it.

Milly was hovering over a water lily. She saw them coming and went over to greet them. "Hello, Billy," she said in her sweet, soft voice. "You look tired, I have heard you have been very busy! Why, the whole kingdom has little else to talk about. You know you are a hero, don't you?"

Billy looked at Milly; he was confused. "A hero?" he asked. "How can that be? Heroes are grown-ups, I have not done anything to be called that."

Now Milly was confused. "Billy, how can you think such a thing? You have saved the entire kingdom, who knows what would have happened to us if the farm had sold?"

Billy said, "No, Milly, I did not save the kingdom or the farm. It was King Augustus and the army that did it. I only told them what was happening. The king is the hero, not me, I only hope to get to see you all whenever I am at the farm."

Awryn looked at Billy. "What do you mean 'whenever you are at the farm'? Where else would you be?"

Billy said, "It is time for me to go to my home, summer is over. The days will soon be getting cooler, and it will be getting dark very early."

Awryn said, "Where will you go, Billy? I do not understand." She had been so happy; now suddenly she felt very sad.

Billy said, "It is time for me to go home, Awryn. School will be starting soon."

"School? What is school? I do not understand why you have to go away."

"Humans my age have to go to school . . . a place to learn about history and math and how to read and write . . . you know, human stuff. I don't want to go to school, but everybody has to go. But don't worry, I'll be back, Awryn, as soon as Christmas break. There will be snow on the ground the next time I come to visit."

"I still don't understand," Awryn said. "When will you leave?"

"Tomorrow morning. My mom is already here. She is waiting on me now."

"Oh, Billy, we have had such fun. How can it be, how can you be leaving?"

Billy said, "I do not want to leave, Awryn. That is just how it always is. I am only here for the summer break and Christmas break every year. I live in the city."

"In the city? What is a city?" asked Awryn.

Billy said, "It is nothing like here, Awryn. Let's not talk about all this now. Do you think we can see the king to tell him the news?"

Awryn had forgotten how happy she had just been and what a hurry she had been in to tell everyone the official news. Her spirits soon began to lift again at the thought of how relieved everyone would be. She knew they would be so relieved that they would surely have a celebration! Yes, a celebration. "Yes, Billy," she said. "Come, hurry, we have to get to Father quickly."

Billy walked to the water's edge, and just as it had done before, the castle began to rise out of the water. As the water cleared off the path, Billy began walking towards the great castle that glistened as the water ran down the walls. Awryn, Billy Bug, and Buzz flew by his side. Billy's steps were so light it seemed he was barely touching the ground himself. The drawbridge began to slowly lower. Billy thought to himself, *I'm not even afraid this time.* Inside the great hall was filled with activity, and there were two rows of dragonfly guards, one on each side of the path leading up to the throne where King Augustus sat. He looked very stern as he was listening intently to Sarge, who seemed to have quite a lot to say. Billy told Awryn, "I think we have come at a bad time."

Then the king saw them approaching, and he looked almost happy to see them. "Come forward, Billy," he said in his deep voice that seemed to make everything in the great hall begin to shake.

Suddenly Billy was very nervous. He slowly approached King Augustus and noticed Billy Bug and Buzz had both hidden in his pocket. He peeked in and saw them both looking at him bug-eyed.

King Augustus looked at Billy and said, "Hello, Billy, I did not expect to see you so soon. Did you enjoy your ride on Lassiter? I saw that he left you at the cotton mill."

Billy said, "Oh yes, King Augustus, everything you and everyone have done for me and Grandma has been great. That is why I am here. You did it, King Augustus, you and the army and all the cotton!"

The wise old king looked at Billy and said, "Billy, you have come here today as if you are in debt to the fairy kingdom and the army of bugs. You are wrong." Billy was feeling sick and queasy, like he was about to get a bellyache. He noticed the palms of his hands were feeling sticky and wet.

Then the king spoke again. "Billy, it is the entire fairy kingdom that is in debt to you, young man. If you had not had the courage to come in and learn about us, we would never have had the opportunity to learn of the danger that threatened all of our existence. The entire kingdom could have fallen if not for you. Please step forward, Billy, I have something for you."

Billy's legs were trembling, and he was not sure if they would work. He still had the bag of penny candy clenched tightly in his hand as he stepped forward.

The King looked directly into Billy's eyes and lifted his great scepter and lowered it to gently tap each of Billy's shoulders, then he said, "Billy, you are now a Knight of the Fairy Kingdom. You may come and go as you please. We all hope that you will come often, and go in peace."

Billy had never felt so good about himself. For the first time he felt comfortable inside the walls of the fairy kingdom. He looked around and saw his friends, Awryn, Milly, Billy Bug, and Buzz. They were all smiling, and Billy suddenly felt like laughing out loud. Then he remembered he was still standing directly before the king. He said, "I also have something for all of you." He held out the wrinkled brown bag of candy and said, "It is candy. It is sweet and my favorite thing to eat. I hope you all like it too."

The king said, "Prepare the dining hall and assemble the troops. Come, Billy, we will all gather around the table in the dining hall and try this 'candy' you speak of."

The king then stood and stepped down from the throne and led the way to the great ceremonial dining hall. When they entered the room, there was a great long table that seemed to go on forever. Billy was not quite sure if he could even see the other end of it. Then the army began arriving, and the great room began to buzz with all the noise and activity. The king took his place at the head of the table and motioned for Billy to sit directly by his side. Sarge had arrived and sat directly across from Billy. Billy Bug and Buzz hopped out of Billy's shirt pocket and began to fly around. They scrambled to get seats close to Billy. Awryn sat beside Sarge. The king held the bag of candy, which now seemed huge as everyone was so small compared to Billy.

As the king stood, the room quieted, and everyone turned to listen to the kind and wise old king. He lifted the paper bag and announced that Billy had brought forth a bounty for the entire kingdom to share. Billy wiggled and squirmed in his seat; he thought a bag of penny candy was hardly a bounty fit for such a kingdom and hardly worthy of a great king to mention. All at the table seemed very interested in what the paper bag could contain. Billy was suddenly nervous again; what if there was not enough?

A silver platter was placed before the king. As he emptied the candy from the bag, Billy became more nervous. What could he have been thinking? Why did he do such things? The platter slowly filled with a mound of candy. There were *hot* jawbreakers, banana taffy, all flavors of bubblegum, and suckers. All of Billy's favorites. The king passed the platter to Sarge, and so it went around the table until it finally made its way back to Billy. Billy looked at the plate; it was still almost full. How could that be? Did the army and the others not want any candy at all? Billy looked down the table and there they all were, laughing and joking with each other, smacking and licking their lips. Bubbles were being blown so big that some of them were lifting out of their chairs. Everyone seemed as if they could not believe the treat that had been given to them.

Billy Bug looked over at Billy and said, "See, Billy, there is nothing to be afraid of if we all work together." Billy felt like Billy Bug was right and at that moment anything was possible and everything was right.

Buzz squeezed between them and said, "Yeah, Billy, see I told you all along everything was going to be all right, you just have to have a little faith!"

All Billy Bug could do was shake his head. He could not stand it any longer and said, "Hey, Buzz, I think Milly wants you to teach her how to blow a bubble."

Buzz looked at Billy Bug and said, "You know, Billy Bug, I think she is attracted to you!"

"Yeah right!" Billy Bug said. "I do have that effect on the ladies."

"OK, you two," Billy said, "I gotta get back to the house. My mom just got here, and I am sure she is wondering about what is going on and where I ran off to in such a hurry."

Awryn looked over at Billy with a concerned look on her face. She felt things were changing and out of her control, although she was not sure why she was feeling this way.

Chapter Thirty-Four

The Farm Is Safe

The king saw that Billy was ready to leave, so he made one final announcement. He thanked Billy for the feast he had provided. Everyone stood and clapped and said thanks to Billy, as they had never had anything that tasted so wonderful. Billy told them all they were welcome and promised to bring them all candy again the next time he came. Mostly he wanted to thank them for all they had done. He felt they surely must not realize what a wonderful gift they had given to him. Grandma and Jake knew the farm was safe now, and he could come back anytime. They would all be there waiting for him and to welcome him back. As he turned to leave the great hall, Awryn, Billy Bug, and Buzz all followed him out. Billy turned and gave a farewell wave to all the others. He was surprised to see the look of sadness in their eyes, and it made him feel the same sadness in his heart. He suddenly remembered what Grandma had said. He waved at everyone and said, "My Grandma is grateful to you all. She doesn't know about you, she just said to thank you for her." With that, he took a deep breath and walked out of the great hall.

There was a boat waiting for him at the drawbridge.

It was made of wood and had curlicue scrolls carved on each end. There was a fairy he had never met before standing in the center of the boat with a great oar that had a paddle on each end. Awryn, Billy Bug, and Buzz all left with him. Billy was glad. He felt to have left the fairy kingdom without his friends might have been more than he could bear.

As they all got into the boat, Billy was very careful as he noticed his weight was the only one that seemed to make any difference. The fairy slowly paddled for the other shore, and Billy felt a great heaviness in his heart. Awryn, Billy Bug, and Buzz were unusually quiet. The only sound was the great oar cutting into the water. The sadness was only growing with the lack of noise, but as luck would have it, there was a grateful break to the silence as Buzz said, "Well, Billy, what's next?"

Billy was surprised. He was caught up so deeply in the moment. He did not know how to tell Billy Bug and Buzz he would soon be leaving to go home, a home so different than the farm. He took a deep breath and said, "I've got to go home, my mom has already come to pick me up. We will be leaving in the morning, right after breakfast."

This bit of information caused all the others to take a deep breath as well. "Leaving tomorrow, so soon?" Awryn said with surprise. "But, Billy, we have only had such a short time together. I feel like I have barely gotten to know you." Her heart was already feeling the emptiness as her mind raced for the million things she wanted to say, but it already seemed too late.

Billy Bug said, "I can come with you. Why not—there is nothing to hold me here."

Buzz said, "Yeah, I can come with you, there is nothing to hold me here."

Billy Bug thought, *Great, I cannot get away from this guy.*

Billy said, "Now hold on, you guys, there is no way you can come with me. I live in the city. It is not like going to town, it is the city!"

Billy Bug said, "Oh come on, Billy, it can't be that bad. I am sure we can make it there, as a matter of fact, there are plenty more just like us there. Why, I would bet we even have relatives that live in the city."

Buzz said, "Yeah, I bet we even have relatives that live in the city."

Billy Bug sighed. *How could I spend another minute with Buzz? Let alone embark on a big adventure to the city?* he thought.

Awryn spoke up and her voice was shaky; they could not help but notice, and it made them all sad as well. "Billy, you know I cannot come, my father would never allow it. I have already done so much this summer that I have never dared to do before. How can I stay here without any of you?"

Billy did not know what to say and did not understand why he felt so sad. What seemed like just a short time ago, they had all been so happy and so relieved. Billy said, "Awryn, this is your home. I wish it were mine. You get to live here all the time. The air is so clean and the river is close. You can lie around in the shade of the big cottonwood trees anytime you want and imagine you are in faraway kingdoms and just think about what you want to do next."

This was not helping Awryn; her feeling of sadness was growing by the second. She wanted to stay with them all as long as she could. She felt like she could not bear to be here in this place for another moment. She could not say good-bye. She could not say anything. The sadness was too great. She took a small step in the air, and before any of them knew it, she had zipped back to the canopy of the tree, with only a faint trail of fairy dust following her.

Chapter Thirty-Five

A Sensitive Bug

Billy looked at Billy Bug and Buzz. None of them knew what to say, so they did not speak. Billy squeezed through the secret opening in the old tree and started up the hill to Grandma's house. When they reached the top, he could not help but look back at the tree. Up in the tree's canopy he saw a flash of light like the sparkle of a diamond. He knew it must be Awryn. It was Awryn; Billy had no way of knowing that the flash was Awryn's tiny tear that had finally fallen. He raised his hand and waved good-bye and said to himself, "I'll see you soon, Awryn. I'll be back before you know it."

Billy Bug and Buzz were hovering nearby. Billy Bug could sense the great sadness, and Buzz could not stand it. He had completely broken down, and his tears were falling freely, making little sprinkles fall from the sky.

Billy Bug said, "Oh come on, Buzz, that is not going to help anything. Why do you have to get so emotional?"

Buzz said, "You know I am a sensitive bug," as he wiped his nose on his arm. "Nothing like you, you think and act like you're so tough. Even though you know that I know you are not, Billy Bug."

"This is no time to start with me," said Billy Bug.

Buzz replied, "I'm not starting anything with you, Mr. Billy Tough Bug."

Billy Bug took a swing at Buzz. Buzz darted behind Billy, and soon they were both buzzing around Billy's head.

Billy shooed them away and said, "Come on, you guys, let's get going."

Chapter Thirty-Six

Of Course They Are Coming

The screen door slammed shut behind Billy as he went into the kitchen; he could hear his mother and Grandma talking. They both stopped and looked up at him. Grandma said, "Well, there you are, Billy. How about some lunch? I can make it for you while you get started with packing your things." The house always seemed so quiet on the day to go back home.

Billy's mom said, "Come on, Billy, I'll help you gather your things, and we can start taking them out to the car." They went back to the room across from Grandma's. "What's this, Billy?" His mom was looking at the jar beside Billy's bed.

"Oh that is the jar I first put Billy Bug in. He usually just stays outside now. I guess that's how it should be anyway, huh, Mom."

She smiled. "I know you will miss him and Buzz. Your Grandma has told me a little about them. Maybe on the ride back to the city you can tell me all about them and your summer. I really can't wait to hear, Billy. I hope you know how proud we all are of you. To think, Mom could have lost her farm if not for you."

"Aw, it was not just me; mostly not me as a matter of fact. I had a lot of help. Grab that jar I'm gonna put Billy Bug and Buzz in it before we go."

"What? Why, Billy? Surely you know you cannot take them with us. It would not be fair to them," his Mom said.

"Of course they are coming. They are already planning on it. Don't worry, Mom, they will come back with me for Christmas break. I'm gonna take my bag out. Do you see anything I missed?"

She was standing at the window. The wind gently blew in, causing the curtains to billow. She breathed deeply to take in as much of the air and the smell of the country as she could. She was thinking of when she was a little girl looking out that window, remembering the sound of the rooster crowing at daybreak. She turned around and looked over the room. "Oh, don't forget your shoes, Billy." They were sitting in the corner of the room; dust was accumulating on the once-shiny black leather. "Why, Billy, your good shoes—I do not think you ever put them on this entire summer."

"Not much need for good shoes, Mom, not even for church on Sunday. Grandma says as long as I was clean that was good enough." He scooped up the shoes and said, "Guess I can always wear them when I go back to school."

They picked up the bags and took them out to the car. Shep saw them coming out of the house and began to prance around and act like a puppy. Billy said, "Aw now, Shep, you know I gotta go. Come here boy . . . shake." Shep raised his paw; Billy took it and said, "You be good while I'm away. Look after the farm and Grandma."

Billy went back inside. Grandma said, "Come on in and sit down, Billy, I've got lunch ready. Jake should be here anytime. You can go ahead and get started."

Billy ate his lunch, but he did not feel much like eating. He was all mixed up; he did not want to go, but he wanted to go and get it over with. Jake came in and sat down at the table; he had just washed his hands, and now he took his hat off and used his handkerchief to wipe the sweat from his forehead. He sighed and said, "Gonna be another hot day." He looked at Billy. "Guess you'll be leaving soon. Sure do hate to see you go. You are getting to be quite the farmhand." He picked up his sandwich and took a big bite—bologna and cheese with mustard. Grandma poured him some cold water out of the pitcher she always kept in the refrigerator.

"I'll be back before you know it, and it will be cool outside then."

"Cool? Why, there will be snow on the ground for sure," Jake said. "Sounds good right about now, and I sure don't like the cold weather." Jake finished his lunch, and they all got up to go outside. Billy stopped by his room and grabbed the jar still sitting on the little table beside his bed.

Jake was just finishing up loading the car. Billy took the lid off the jar, and Billy Bug and Buzz flew in. Billy held the jar up to eye level and said, "OK, guys, you sure you're ready for this?"

Billy Bug was all smiles and ready for the big adventure. Buzz looked sad and was just about to tear up. Billy took the jar lid off and looked down in the jar. "Hey, Buzz, what's the matter?"

Buzz looked up at Billy and said, "I do not want to go to the city, but I do not want to stay either."

Billy Bug looked at Buzz and said, "Oh come on, we are about to leave, you bug me."

Buzz said, "Why do you gotta be mean to me? You know I do not feel good."

Billy said, "OK, come on out, Buzz." Buzz flew up and sat on the rim of the jar. "Now, Buzz, you gotta make up your own mind about this because there will not be any changing it after we leave."

Billy Bug said, "Just stay, Buzz. If you come you will just be moping around and miserable."

Buzz knew he was right but did not care much what Billy Bug thought at the moment. "All right, I am not going. I am gonna stay here and keep Awryn company. I know *she* enjoys *my* company." He glared at Billy Bug.

"Well, finally you make the right decision about something. Adios, sayonara, farewell, see you later." Billy Bug would never admit that he was going to miss Buzz. Knowing that he was the only one going, he was beginning to wonder if he had made the right choice.

Buzz looked at Billy. "You know I am going to miss you like crazy."

"It's OK, Buzz, I am glad you are going to stay with Awryn, I know it will make her feel better. We will be back before you know it." Buzz flew off the rim and flew down to look inside the glass at Billy Bug. "And you know, I am not going to miss you at all. Don't you worry, I will be here taking care of everything, like I always do."

"You do that, Buzz. I am sure we will hear all about it, more than we want to know, as soon as we get back."

"Yeah, you're going to hear about it, more than you want to!"

Billy Bug just shook his head. With that, Buzz did a full backflip in flight and zipped away towards the bottom of the hill. Billy looked down in the jar at Billy Bug. "You OK?" he asked.

"Of course. Good riddance. I am glad he is staying, he shouldn't have even thought about coming in the first place. All he would have done was mope around and make us all crazy."

Billy screwed the lid on the jar; Billy Bug swallowed hard. He suddenly had a big lump in his throat. Billy's mom was getting in the car. Grandma and Jake were saying their final good-byes to her, and then they both looked at Billy.

Grandma said, "I don't know why it is always so sad to see you go, we know you'll be back as soon as school lets out for Christmas break."

Jake said, "You know we'll have plenty of time to have fun, no working in the garden!" He opened the door for Billy to get in;

Billy hopped in and rolled down the window and sat Billy Bug in the back glass so he could see where they were going, or at least where they had been.

As they pulled out onto the dirt road, Billy looked out of the window; summer was already fading. The next time he would see the farm there would be waist-high winter snowdrifts on both sides of the road. He would walk through them like a plow. *Better not forget my galoshes,* he thought. Shep was running alongside the car but getting tired as the car pulled away. Billy turned and waved. He and his new friends had saved the farm.

Made in the USA
Las Vegas, NV
16 November 2020

10988629R20074